STACY McANULTY

RANDOM HOUSE
NEW YORK

THE

MISCALCULATIONS

OF

LIGHTNING

GIRL

Text copyright © 2018 by Stacy McAnulty
Jacket art copyright © 2018 by Jim Tierney
Book design by Maria T. Middleton

Math problem on p. 208 printed with permission from the Mathematical Association of America. To learn more about the Putnam Competition, visit amc.maa.org.

Photo on p. 286 © iStock.com/joingate

Visit us on the Web! rhcbooks.com

Educators and librarians, for a variety of teaching tools, visit us at RHTeachersLibrarians.com

Library of Congress Cataloging-in-Publication Data
Names: McAnulty, Stacy, author.
Title: The Miscalculations of Lightning Girl / Stacy McAnulty.
Description: First edition. | New York: Random House, [2018] | Summary: A lightning strike made Lucy, twelve, a math genius, but after years of homeschooling, her grandmother enrolls her in middle school and she learns that life is more than numbers.
Identifiers: LCCN 2017021152 | ISBN 978-1-5247-6757-0 (hardcover) | ISBN 978-1-5247-6758-7 (hardcover library binding) | ISBN 978-0-525-64457-6 (int'l) | ISBN 978-1-5247-6759-4 (ebook)
Subjects: | CYAC: Savants (Savant syndrome)—Fiction. | Obsessive-compulsive disorder—Fiction. | Middle schools—Fiction. | Schools—Fiction. | Interpersonal relations—Fiction.
Classification: LCC PZ7.M47825255 Mis 2018 | DDC [Fic]—dc23

Printed in the United States of America
10 9 8 7 6 5 4 3 2 1
First Edition

For Cora,
finally!

I don't remember the moment that changed my life 4 years ago. Call it a side effect of being struck by lightning. That bolt of electricity burned a small hole in my memory. It also rewired my brain, transforming me into Lucille Fanny Callahan, math genius.

I've been told the lightning-strike story 42 times, so it's almost like my own memory. I see it perfectly: I'm at the Crystal Creek Apartments, where Nana and I lived then. (There's not really a creek, just a big dirty fountain in front.) I'm playing outside with a girl named Cecelia when the thunderstorm starts. We live in North Carolina, and storms happen all the time in the spring and summer. We watch from behind a toolshed. For some reason,

I climb on the chain link fence. Maybe 8-year-old me was a daredevil; 12-year-old me definitely is not.

Lightning strikes the fence, and the electricity runs through the metal links and then through me. Some of the current even jumps from me to Cecelia. I'm knocked out. Cecelia is just knocked over. She runs and gets help. Joe, the maintenance man, uses a defibrillator on me because the electricity from the lightning stopped my heart. The electricity from the defibrillator starts it back up.

I do remember the hospital and the black burns on my pale hands. I remember pretending to be asleep while Nana prayed next to my bed. I only stayed in the hospital 1 night. The doctors did all their tests. They said my heart took a 2- to 5-minute nap. (I hate that no one knows the exact number.) They said I was lucky and I'd be fine. Back to normal in a few days. But doctors are wrong sometimes.

A week later, Nana and I were watching TV, and a commercial came on for a used-car dealership. The man was screaming, so I had to pay attention.

"That's $359 a month for 48 months, folks." He was really loud. "Nobody beats Frank Fontana. Nobody."

I yelled back, "17,232."

"What?" Nana asked.

"That's how much the car costs," I said.

"Did you read it on the TV?"

"I just know. 359 times 48 is 17,232."

Nana frowned and shook her head. But then she got up and went to find a calculator.

"What were those numbers again?" she asked.

I told her, and she punched them in. "And the answer?"

"17,232."

"You're right." She sounded surprised. I wasn't surprised, but I guess I should have been. I mean, I was only in 2nd grade, and we were still learning addition and subtraction.

Nana turned off the television.

"What's 99 times 88?" she asked.

"8,712. Can we have McDonald's for dinner?" I asked.

Nana ignored me and asked another math problem and then another. She kept using bigger numbers, more digits. But it never got harder.

The doctors call my condition acquired savant syndrome. *Savant* means that my math skills are far beyond normal, and *acquired* means I wasn't born with this wacky ability. I got it because I was holding a metal fence during a lightning storm. Cecelia didn't get any special powers. We stopped being friends soon after that. I was busy trying to understand my new brain, and in the fall Nana and I moved.

Acquired savant syndrome is caused by brain damage. I can't say that in front of Nana. She thinks it's a miracle. My uncle Paul likes to think of it as a superpower, something from a comic book or a movie. But really, I'm brain damaged. Part of my left lobe has been turned off, and now my right lobe works overtime.

My condition is really rare. I've never met anyone with it. It's even rarer in females, and superrare in kids. 1 of my doctors, Dr. Emily Bahri, specializes in savant syndrome. She's worked with a lady who can make a drawing so realistic it looks like a photo, and with a guy who can speak any language after hearing it only a few times. I'm her only acquired savant patient. Years ago, Dr. Bahri did have a guy who, after hitting his head on the bottom of a swimming pool, could suddenly play the piano. He'd never taken a single lesson. But that guy is dead now from old age.

My supercomputer brain can do more than add, subtract, multiply, and divide (which is no more impressive than a $3 calculator). I can also do calendar math. January 14, 1901, was a Monday. July 2, 1975, was a Wednesday. September 30, 2055, will be a Thursday. (Google can do this, too, and almost as fast.)

I also *see* math. Every number has its own color and shape. Take the number 5—it's a jelly bean shape, red-brown, like the color of Carolina mud. The number 12 is a set of cream-colored squares. The number 47 is a fluorescent-orange oval. Prime numbers have curves. Non-primes have hard edges.

These colors and shapes make it fun and easy to play

with numbers, and I can find patterns in anything from the stock market to baseball games to the price of cereal. Nana likes to bargain shop.

And then there's my number memory ability. I remember every set of numbers I hear or see, like license plates or phone numbers or the digits of pi (π).

Pi is my favorite mathematical constant. But because the digits of pi after the point go on forever, I only let myself recite the numbers to the 314th decimal place.

π=3.14159265358979323846264338327950288419716939937510582097494459230781640628620899862803482534211706798214808651328230664709384460955058223172535940812848111745028410270193852110555964462294895493038196442881097566593344612847564823378678316527120190914564856692346034861045432664821339360726024914127372458700660631

These digits repeat in my brain even when I don't want them to. It's like getting a song stuck in your head. Only for me, it's always the same song. Incredibly annoying, but still beautiful.

Being a savant does have its downsides. Like the guy who hit his head in the pool and could play the piano? He was blind after the accident. I'm not blind, but I do have my own issues. When people meet me, they expect Einstein or Maryam Mirzakhani (if they're familiar with recent mathematical geniuses). But instead, they get the 1 and only freaky-strange Lucy. The girl who can't sit down without making you stare at her because she needs to do it 3 times. The girl who would rather calculate your age down to the hour than talk about your hobbies. The girl who never leaves the house without a supply of Clorox wipes and hand sanitizer.

Lucky for me—and everybody else—I rarely have to meet people. I'm a reclusive genius.

Nana and I sit on the couch and pretend we aren't waiting for the doorbell. Uncle Paul said sometime after 4:00 p.m. It's only 4:11. So, technically, he's not late, and he won't ever be, even if he doesn't show up for days.

We watch a game show where people run around a grocery store. I like game shows. There are always points or prices to calculate.

A knock. Finally.

I'm off the couch and opening the apartment door before Nana gets up.

Uncle Paul stands in the doorway with a duffel bag.

He's wearing regular clothes—T-shirt, jeans, sneakers—not his marine uniform.

"There she is." He drops the bag. "My favorite genius and future Nobel Prize winner."

I jump into his arms. "I missed you." He smells like soap and trees. "And there's no Nobel Prize for math. I'm going to win the Fields Medal." I've told him this before. I think he forgets on purpose.

When I let go, Nana moves in for her hug. Her gray-blond head doesn't even reach his shoulders.

"Hey, Ma." He squeezes her so tight her feet come off the floor.

As he steps into the living room, I offer him a squirt of hand sanitizer from the bottle I keep by the door. I use some, too.

"Thanks." He looks around the apartment. Nana and I have only lived here since January. 193 days.

Nana pulls Uncle Paul to the couch. She studies him like she's checking for damage. He looks the same to me, except his white skin is red from the sun.

I take the chair, giving them some space.

I sit.

Then stand.

Then sit.

Then stand.

And finally sit.

"You still do your funny dance," Uncle Paul says.

"Don't tease her." Nana squeezes his arm.

"I'm not teasing. It's cute. Like the way she used to say spaghetti. Pa-sket-ee." He winks at me.

"I can say spaghetti fine." Now that my front teeth have grown in. But I can't *just* sit down, or stand still.

"So...," Nana says, asking a question she can't put into words.

"I'm going to Twentynine Palms. In California."

"Oh, thank God." She makes the sign of the cross and folds her hands in a quick prayer. Usually, her prayers are much longer. Like when she was praying Uncle Paul wouldn't have to go back to the Middle East. He's already been to Afghanistan twice.

"That's a great name," I say. "You're going to live in a prime number." I'd like to live in a town that has a number in its name. There is a Five Points, North Carolina. But Nana says we can't move 2 hours away because I love the name.

"Prime number, huh? Must be a sign. Right, Ma?" He winks at her.

Nana likes when the universe gives her signals that good things are coming.

Uncle Paul tells us about his new post and his girlfriend, who lives near D.C. He shows us pictures on his phone—mostly of the girlfriend. He gives Nana a silk scarf and a bag of her favorite licorice from the base commissary—it's German. I get a lightning-bolt charm on a silver chain.

"Lightning. It's your good-luck symbol." Uncle Paul helps me put it on. "What doesn't kill you makes you stronger. Right?"

"I wouldn't recommend getting struck. Lightning kills an average of 47 people in America every year and severely injures hundreds, maybe thousands." To my disappointment, the government only keeps an accurate count of those who die.

"Good to know," he says. "Do you not want the necklace?"

"No, I love it. Thank you." I rub the charm between my finger and thumb. It needs to be wiped with Clorox, but that seems rude. I do it anyway.

"So, ladies, what's happening here on the home front?" he asks. "But wait. 1st, Lucy, how old am I?"

"11,881 days."

"And?"

I look at the clock. "19 hours, 7 minutes."

He laughs. If it were anyone else, I'd be insulted he thinks my math skills are some kind of party trick.

"You're freakin' amazing."

"Watch your language," Nana warns.

"I *was* watching my language." He kisses her cheek. "Sorry, Ma. Now, seriously, what have you been up to?"

"I just graduated from high school."

"Really? You're only 10."

"I'm 12."

"Impressive." He gives me a thumbs-up.

"An impressive exaggeration," Nana says. "Shouldn't you *go* to high school before graduating from high school?"

I roll my eyes, though Nana is sort of right. I didn't technically do every grade and every class.

"I've finished all the homeschool requirements. I've passed the GED and—"

"She got a perfect score on her SATs." Nana finishes my thought.

"Yes! Well, on the math section." I did okay with the reading and writing parts.

Nana shakes her head. "She's a good test taker."

"Congrats, Luce. What's next for the young genius? Harvard?"

"Don't get her started," Nana says.

"I want to take college classes online. I mean ... well, I've been taking them for 2 semesters already, but under Nana's name. For fun."

"I have 15 college credits." Nana sits up straighter.

"But now I can take them in my own name."

"That's amazing, Luce. Maybe you could go to NC State. That's where I would have gone if I was smart like you."

"She's not going anywhere," Nana says. "Can you imagine a 12-year-old living in the dorms?"

"But I can do everything online. If Nana will let me."

She breathes out a loud sigh. "You can't do *everything* online."

"Whatever." I don't want to have this argument again.

Uncle Paul looks at Nana and then at me. "What's going on?"

"Nana wants me to go to public school."

"She's too smart for regular school. I went to regular school." Uncle Paul acts like he's not smart, but that isn't true. He knows geography and history better than anyone I've ever met. He's really good at *Jeopardy!* I kept track of his score last time we watched. He had $11,500.

Nana shakes her head again. "Ask her when was the last time she left this apartment."

"Lucy," Uncle Paul mocks Nana's voice. "When was the last time you left this apartment?"

I shrug, pretending not to know the answer.

"Lucille?" he says.

"About 4 weeks ago." That sounds better than 32 days ago. I had an appointment with my brain doctor on June 25.

Nana sighs. "See."

"Maybe I'm wrong."

Nana laughs. "That would be a 1st."

Uncle Paul doesn't laugh. "You can't stay holed up in

this apartment. What about friends? What about fresh air? She probably has a vitamin D deficiency."

"I have friends, and I get plenty of vitamin D. I take a gummy vitamin every morning."

"How many?" Nana asks.

"Vitamins?"

"Friends?"

"Um…" This is actually a hard answer to calculate. What makes someone a friend? A shared interest? Is there a minimum amount of time you need to spend together? Does the other person need to call you a friend, too?

Nana rubs the back of her neck. "I think this is the real—"

"4!" I shout. "I have 4 friends."

"Who?" Nana asks.

"SquareHead314, HipHypotenuse, Numberlicious, and GregS77."

"What?" Nana laughs, but I'm not joking. "Are those people?"

"Yes, they're online friends. I know them from the math forums and the tutoring websites."

"Do you know anything about them?" Uncle Paul asks, shaking his head. My family is ganging up on me.

"I know SquareHead314 is a whiz with differential equations. He … or she … can explain things in the simplest terms."

"He or she?" Uncle Paul asks.

"Don't be sexist. Girls are as good at math as boys are. I can't assume SquareHead314 is a boy." Now it's my turn to shake my head.

"SquareHead is not your friend if you don't even know his ... her ... gender." Uncle Paul runs his hands over his microshort (maybe ⅛ inch) hair.

"What do you want me to do? Nana told me to be careful on the Internet. I try not to ask personal questions."

"Lucy, you don't know these people. You've never met them. They're not your friends," Nana says.

"Do you want me to invite them over?"

"No!" Nana snaps. "These people could be murderers. Especially Greg77. He obviously has no imagination."

"It's Greg-S-77. And he's an expert in string theory."

"What is that?" She holds up a hand. "Never mind."

"Ma, how did you let this happen?" Uncle Paul asks. "Lucy needs to be around other kids. You can't keep her locked away."

"That's right. I have her locked in a tower and never let her out. She'll have to grow her hair and escape through the window if she ever wants to leave. Please, Paul."

This would be a good time for me to say, *Don't blame Nana. Sure, she is the 1 who pulled me out of elementary school after 2nd grade. But I've never wanted to go back. Nana tried. She forced me to go to the homeschool gym class at the Y last year. I hated it. The other kids hated*

it, too. I only like to bounce a basketball 3 times. Or jump
rope 3 times. Or run around the track 3 times. Actually, I
hate running around the track any number of times. Peo-
ple don't get me, and I don't really need the distractions.

Instead, I say, "Nana hasn't been to her doctor in over
2 years. 741 days exactly."

"What!" Paul says.

"What does that have to do with anything?"

"Ma, you have to take care of yourself."

Nana and Uncle Paul go back and forth. I quietly excuse myself and carry Uncle Paul's duffel bag to my bedroom. I'm letting him sleep there for the weekend.

I log on to my computer.

LightningGirl: Hey, friends. I'm back.

**SquareHead314: Great. We're talking fractal
geometry.**

Maybe SquareHead and the others aren't *friend*
friends. But we've got a shared love of math. Maybe that's
enough.

Life is like an equation, and mine is perfectly bal-
anced.

Nana + Uncle Paul + Math = Happiness

Other people might need to add in friends or sports
or money or something else, but my equation is already solved.

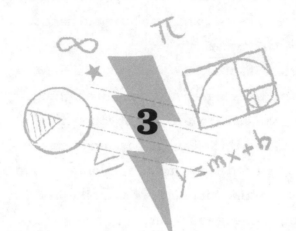

Uncle Paul stays with us for 3 nights. I hate that he's about to leave—even though he forced me out of the apartment every day while he was here. We've gone for ice cream, gone to the movies, bought groceries, and gone bowling. He bowled. I watched.

I give Uncle Paul a hug in the parking lot. Nana and I don't know when we'll see him again. But I am happy to get my room back, and my bed. Nana kicks in her sleep. It's like she's on a treadmill.

"I'm going to miss you, genius." He kisses my cheek. "Be good for the old lady."

"Who are you calling old?" Nana gives him a hug, then a kiss, then another hug and another kiss.

"Okay, okay, Ma. You're turning into Lucy."

"Very funny," I say.

Nana and I watch Uncle Paul get into his Jeep and drive off. He waves an arm through the open window. Nana wipes her eye with her thumb.

I turn to go back inside, but she grabs my elbow.

"Get in the car," she says.

"What? Why?" I notice that Nana has her purse.

"Just get in."

"I don't have my wipes or hand sanitizer."

She pats her bag. "Get in."

I sit, stand, sit, stand, sit in the front seat, which is harder to do in the car than in the living room. When I close the door, Nana presses the door-lock button.

"Where are we going?"

"You'll see," she says.

The car radio plays country music. Nana sings along, even though she doesn't seem to know any of the words. I stare out the window and count the telephone poles.

We drive past BI LO and Cracker Barrel, where Nana works, and the Route 68 Diner (my favorite place to eat because it has a great name and great curly fries).

I've counted 117 telephone poles and 3 traffic lights when Nana turns on her blinker, and I see the sign.

EAST HAMLIN MIDDLE SCHOOL.

"Why are we here?"

She parks in a lot that has only 7 cars.

"Let's go," Nana says.

I can't move. Nana gets out and walks around to my side. She yanks open my door, reaches across me, and takes off my seat belt.

"I will carry you," she threatens.

I know she can't lift me with her bad back, and I'm already taller than she is. I also know that we aren't leaving until she gets what she wants.

"Tell me why we are here," I say without looking at her.

She sighs. "My darling genius granddaughter...don't play dumb with me."

"I'm not."

"You're going to middle school," she says.

"I should be going to college," I snap. *Or at least high school.*

"I don't think so. You need to work on some of your soft skills before I send you off to MIT. You need to be around your peers. Now, come on." She kisses her palm and pats it to my forehead. Then she starts walking toward the 2-story building. I have no choice but to follow. She's going to sign me up even if I stay in the car.

The best decision Nana ever made was taking me out of public school. Now she wants to send me back. Obviously, her judgment is deteriorating.

After I was diagnosed as a savant, school got really hard for me. Not the work. I basically bothered my 2nd-grade teacher all day long asking for more math problems. She gave me an old high school textbook and sat me in the back of the classroom. That worked for a while. Until the day we celebrated her 60th birthday in class.

"You're 21,915 days old," I shouted after she blew out the candle on her cupcake.

"Wow," Mrs. Chew said. "That's a lot of days." She was used to me throwing out numbers and calculating everything. She was no longer impressed.

"And if you die when you're 80, that's in 7,305 days. And it'll be a Sunday."

"That's enough of that talk," Mrs. Chew warned. Then she went to the supply closet to get paper towels because Carter Harrison got frosting in his hair.

"Hey, Lucy, how many days until I die?" Rachel McKey asked.

I looked at the wall where all our birthdays were written on cake-slice cutouts.

"If you die when you're 80, you have 26,405 days to go," I explained.

"What about me?" Carter asked.

I did a quick calculation. "You'll die in 26,202 days."

Then I had to tell everyone exactly how long I expected them to live. Really, I was just calculating the days until they turned 80. (Some of them would probably die before 80.) But Rachel started crying when she heard her best friend, Sofia Garcia, would outlive her by 172 days.

"What's going on?" Mrs. Chew demanded.

"Lucy's telling us when we're going to die," Rachel said. Her eyes were red, and her nose was running.

"You asked."

Mrs. Chew sent me to the main office. And that wasn't the 1st time. By the end of the year, Nana had had enough. "She spends more time with the principal than in the classroom!" she yelled. If Nana had bothered to do the math, she'd have found that, technically, that wasn't true. Still, she pulled me out of school and didn't make me go back. I got to stay in our apartment all day, learning some stuff from Nana and then mostly from my computer. 1,508 days of studying from the comfort of my bedroom. Looks like those days are over.

When we get to the main office of East Hamlin Middle, it's obvious that Nana hasn't really thought this through. She hasn't made an appointment, and she hasn't brought along any of my records. Not like that's going to stop Nana when she's on a mission.

A secretary gives us a little tour while we wait for the principal. I count the lockers, the stairs, the doors, everything.

"This hallway is mainly 8th grade, but it also has the music rooms. We have band, orchestra, and chorus.

Would you like to see the music rooms?" the secretary asks, sounding bored.

"No thank you." I want this to be over.

The cafeteria doors are propped open. We follow the lady inside. It's the biggest room I've ever seen. We could have fit 6 of my elementary school cafeterias in here. Sunlight shines through the wall of windows, and the dust in the air twinkles. The air-conditioning pushes these particles around, creating a beautiful fractal pattern. I wish I could take a picture of it, but it can only be seen clearly in my brain.

"It's a nice school," Nana says.

"I guess." I tap my toe 3 times.

When the tour's done, Nana and I meet with the principal in his office. On his messy desk is a crystal plaque that says DISTRICT PRINCIPAL OF THE YEAR. He shakes Nana's hand and tells us to have a seat.

I sit, stand, sit, stand, sit in a wooden chair.

Dr. Cobb stares but doesn't say anything.

I wish I could explain it to him. If I don't do this routine, my brain will go into frantic-repeat mode. The digits of pi will take over like an infection. I won't be able to concentrate on anything but the numbers.

Nana pulls out an old receipt from her purse and helps herself to a pen from the principal's desk.

"When's the 1st day of school?" she asks.

"1st day for students is August 27th."

"And what time do classes start?"

"Homeroom begins at 7:30. But let's—"

"School ends at what time?" Nana doesn't let the man talk.

"10 after 2."

"And what grade will Lucy be in?"

"We need to slow down here." Dr. Cobb holds up his hands. "Please, Mrs. Callahan. May I ask a few questions?"

"I'm not going to stop you." She leans back in her chair.

"Great." He smiles wide. "Lucy has been home-schooled for how long?"

1,508 days.

"Since 3rd grade," Nana says.

"And you've been her primary educator?" he asks.

"For the most part. We use a lot of computer resources." Nana smooths my hair. I push her hand away.

"Do you have her records?" he asks. "The state requires attendance, grades, and end-of-year—"

"All A's," Nana interrupts again. "Lucy's very smart. Very, very smart." She doesn't say *genius,* or *savant,* or *prodigy.* She doesn't mention the lightning strike.

"Do you have *any* records?" He folds his hands and puts them on his desk. It's like he already knows the answer.

"I'll email them to you," she says.

Nana hasn't kept any records, but I have. All my grades are neatly organized in a spreadsheet, and I have copies of every test, project, and paper stored in folders.

"We will also need immunization records."

She writes that down. "Anything else?"

"Joyce is getting the rest of the paperwork. You'll find everything in there."

"Good." Nana clicks the pen closed and gives it back to Dr. Cobb.

He looks at me again. "You're 12?"

I nod.

"Well, Lucy, welcome to East Hamlin Middle and to 7th grade." He offers me his hand. I don't shake it.

"Lucy doesn't shake hands," Nana explains. "She's afraid of germs."

That's true. And Nana is forcing me to be part of this germ-infested community where the people are called my peers only because we are the same age. My real peers are creating algorithms and solving problems. They'll be changing the world while I'll be wasting time memorizing textbooks and ducking dodgeballs.

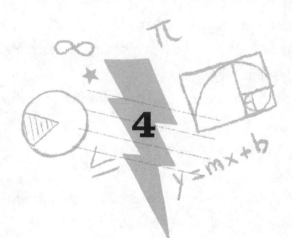

Nana insists on taking a picture on my 1st day of school.

"Why are you doing this to me?" I ask, refusing to smile.

"It's only a picture." She holds up her cell phone.

"That's not what I mean." I'd been hoping that Nana would change her mind about middle school. I refused to give her my records of classes and grades. But she figured out my password (lucy31415; I need to think of something harder) and printed my files. She only took the records through 6th grade, nothing higher.

"Lucy, we've been over this. Give it a year. You can

always start college when you're 13. That's still 5 years earlier than most people."

"There's a 12-year-old boy starting at Cornell this month!"

"Well, he obviously has a nicer grandmother than you do. College can wait."

"It can wait 1 year? That's it, right? Can I get that in writing?" I slide my lightning-bolt necklace under my shirt.

"I promise." She says it too easily. "Give it 1 year and really make a go of it. Make 1 friend. Do 1 thing outside of these walls. Read 1 book not written by an economist or a mathematician."

"1 year, 1 friend, 1 activity, 1 book. This year is brought to you by the number 1." I try to sound like the Count from *Sesame Street*.

"Yes, now smile. You're such a beautiful girl when you smile."

I roll my eyes and stick out my tongue. Nana can't control everything.

She sighs. "I'm going to say an extra prayer for you."

"Thanks. I'm going to need it."

East Hamlin Middle School has SMOD—standard mode of dress. It's not a uniform, just superstrict rules for clothes. Our shirts can only be red, white, or blue. Shorts and pants need to be khaki or dark blue, no jeans. Nana had to go to Walmart to buy me a whole new set of itchy, stiff clothes.

"Why didn't you tell the principal that I'm a genius?" I ask as I put my new lunch bag into my new backpack.

"I told him you were really smart. And they'll figure it out soon enough. In the beginning, I thought you might want to be treated like any other kid." She gives me a hug. "Don't worry. I'm sure there are still some things they can teach you."

Nana offers to wait with me at the bus stop. I want to go alone. I know she's watching from the window. She's making sure I don't hide inside the dumpster or something. Like that would happen.

There are 7 kids at the bus stop in front of our apartment. A prime number. A good sign if you believe in that kind of thing. I recognize them but don't *know* any of them. All of them play on their phones or wear headphones and stare off into space.

I have a phone, too—a back-to-school gift from Nana—but it's just a phone. It can only text and call.

I hear the bus a long time before I see it. When it screeches to a stop, we walk up the 3 steps in a quiet, orderly fashion. The bus driver, a lady about Nana's age, stares straight ahead and doesn't say anything.

I take the 1st open seat I find. I sit. I stand. I sit. I stand. "Sit down!" the bus driver yells.

I sit, relieved that I don't need to do my routine 5

times. That might have landed me in detention or gotten me suspended or something. I don't know a lot about the school district's system of punishment.

I slide over to the window. The bus makes another stop, and 4 kids get on. I watch each of them pass by. The last girl meets my eyes and snarls. She's a pretty girl with long blond hair and blue eyes covered in black eye shadow, but when she snarls, she looks like a rabid raccoon. We had 1 of those once behind our apartment.

I decide to keep my gaze down.

Tomorrow, I'll bring a book or something. Maybe a sudoku puzzle. But they don't take me much time. As fast as I can move the pen, I can fill them in. I even did the 1 created by a mathematician from Finland. He called it the hardest sudoku ever made, with only 23 of the 81 squares filled in at the start. I still finished it in less than 5 minutes.

Everything changes at the 4th stop when a girl falls into the seat next to me. She falls partly on me, too. I push her off as politely as I can.

"Sorry about that," she says.

"It's okay."

She adjusts her glasses up on her face and swings her backpack onto her lap. It's army green (like the number 20) and covered with patches. SAVE THE POLAR BEARS. EQUAL PAY FOR EQUAL WORK. RESPECT MOTHER EARTH.

"I can't believe I used to love the 1st day of school,"

she says. "Like when I was in elementary school. But my sister was right—middle school is ..." She stops and looks around, then she whispers a word Uncle Paul would use to describe a bad night in Afghanistan.

I nod, already agreeing with this girl's sister, and the school day hasn't officially started.

"Are you a 6th grader?" she asks.

"No. 7th."

"You must be new to EHMS. Or you're superquiet, because I don't remember you from last year." She studies me closely.

"I enrolled over the summer. I was supposed to go to another school." *Or college.*

"What school? John Glenn Middle? They had a kid bring a knife to school like 2 years ago, and now my mom thinks it's a gang school."

"Not John Glenn." I shake my head.

"I'm in 7th grade, too. But a lot of people think I'm in high school. The lifeguard at the pool this summer thought I was in 10th grade." She does look older, but 10th grade is a stretch. She has braces and brown hair that flips out at the ends in a spiky way. Hair doesn't normally do that; at least I don't think so. It's definitely cooler than my braid. She has a cluster of pimples across her white forehead that are covered in makeup. She smells like vanilla perfume and wears shiny pink lip gloss.

"What's your name?" she asks.

"What's your name?" I ask back.

"Okay. That's weird." She dramatically lifts her eyebrows.

"Sorry. I'm Lucy."

"I'm Windy. Not Wendy, but Windy. With an *i*." Then she blows in my face. I try not to breathe. I last 10 seconds.

"Are you okay?" she asks.

I suck in another breath. "That wasn't very sanitary."

"Geez, relax. Do you think I'm diseased or something?" I can't tell whether she's trying to be mean or she's just weird. She didn't snarl like the other girl.

"No. But . . ."

"But what?" She glares at me and moves even closer.

"We all carry germs and bacteria. They're everywhere. We each have a cloud of microbes that swim around us. They're called—"

"Microbiomes!" she yells. "I did my science fair experiment last year on microbiomes."

I didn't expect this girl with spiky hair and no concern for personal space to know about microbiomes. As a peace offering, I pull out my bottle of hand sanitizer and offer her a squirt.

She holds out her palm and takes a glob. I use some, too.

"Feel better?" she asks.

I nod.

"Did you know malaria kills 1 child every 30 seconds somewhere in the world?" She raises her eyebrows again. "Malaria is something to be afraid of. Not microbiomes."

That would be 1,051,200 dead children a year.

"Last year I helped raise enough money to send 120 mosquito nets to a village in Ghana," she brags.

"Wow." I don't tell her that she only helped 0.01 percent of the possible malaria victims. Math can be cruel sometimes.

"Who do you have for homeroom?" she asks, suddenly changing topics.

"Room 213." I remember the room number before the teacher's name. "Mr. Stoker."

"Me too. We're on the same team. That's cool."

The bus parks in front of the school before Windy can ask anything else. When the doors open, she pushes into the aisle and disappears. I can't make my way out. At least not without touching anyone. I get off the bus last. Windy's gone, and I'm alone with hundreds of strangers. Someone knocks into me, and I bump into a kid whose microbiome is 90 percent body spray.

"Watch it." He throws his elbow to make space.

I take a breath and realize that hiding in the dumpster would have been a better way to spend the day.

Finding room 213 is easy. Getting in is impossible. From the hall, I tap my toe 3 times and watch 4 kids go to the door. Mr. Stoker shakes hands with each of them before he allows them into his class. He holds their hands for 3 seconds as he speaks to them. He smiles more than the kids do. I assume this is a 1st-day ritual and not something we have to go through each morning. Maybe I should try again tomorrow.

Another student goes in. Then another. Each forced to shake hands with the teacher.

"Hey!" Out of nowhere Windy jumps in front of me. "Sorry I ran off. Needed to use the bathroom before class.

That's what happens when you start the day with 3 cups of coffee."

"You drink coffee?"

"When my mom's not looking. Coffee isn't bad for you. Some people say caffeine stunts your growth, but I'm fine with that. I'd like to stay this size. Plus, I needed a jolt. I stayed up all night listening to *Hamilton*."

"Okay?" I don't mean for it to sound like a question.

"The Tony Award–winning musical," she says. "You know it, right?"

I shake my head. "I'm not into music."

"You should listen to it. Life-changing!"

A bell rings.

"Come on." Windy and her massive backpack head toward Mr. Stoker. I watch her shake the man's hand. It looks so simple, and he appears to be a clean guy. He's tall, with cropped black hair, a thin mustache, and dark brown skin. He wears a bright white shirt with a narrow green tie (the color of the number 38). His dark blue pants (the color of 62) look brand-new. He probably washes regularly. But he's touched the hand of every kid who walked into the room. The exponential magnitude of germ growth is disgusting. I force myself not to estimate the number of bacteria being passed around.

I feel dizzy.

As the hallway clears out, Mr. Stoker notices me.

"Do you need some assistance?" he asks in a friendly store-clerk way.

"No."

"Are you supposed to be in my homeroom?" he asks, still smiling.

"Yes, sir."

"Are you Lucille Callahan?"

I nod. We've never met before. I know that much. Maybe the principal warned him about me. Maybe if I'm late, they'll kick me out of school.

"Your grandmother sent me an email. She said you hadn't been to middle school before. But don't worry; it's a new year for everyone. Except me. This is my 15th year in 7th grade." He motions to the door and then puts his hands in his pockets.

I wonder what else Nana told him. Obviously, she mentioned my phobia

I slowly walk to the door. I keep my eyes on Mr. Stoker to see if he takes out his germy hands. But he just rocks back and forth like he's listening to music.

"Welcome. I'm Mr. Stoker, your homeroom and 1st-period math teacher. Please find your seat. They're labeled. I have 1 question for you. Do you prefer to be called Lucille or Lucy?"

"Lucy."

The moment I step into room 213, I fall in love.

Mr. Stoker has a banner that wraps around all 4 walls with the value of pi to the 280th place. (By the way, it's 2.) And he has posters with equations, and 1 with the Fibonacci sequence. If I had to pick a favorite math sequence, it would be Fibonacci.

0, 1, 1, 2, 3, 5, 8, 13, 21.

Mr. Stoker also has some funny posters. 5 OUT OF 4 PEOPLE DON'T UNDERSTAND FRACTIONS. And another: MATH IS A JOURNEY, SO SHOW YOUR WORK.

"Lucy," Windy half yells, half whispers, and everyone turns to look at me. "That's your seat." She points to a desk in the 2nd row that has a paper with my name written on it.

I try to smile in thanks. And I tap my toe 3 times to keep the numbers quiet and to keep from running out the door.

When I get to my seat, I put my backpack on the floor. Mr. Stoker's at the front of the room, introducing himself again. I don't know what to do 1st, sit down or clean my desk.

"The warning bell rings at 7:25. The 2nd bell at 7:30." Mr. Stoker speaks in a low voice that can only be heard if everyone is quiet. "You're expected to be in your seat, ready to start the day, at 7:30."

I don't think Mr. Stoker's picking on me specifically. But I'm the only person not sitting. I take a breath and sit.

Stay, Lucy.

But I can't. Numbers invade my head.

3.14159 …

Ignore them!

26535897932384626 …

Mr. Stoker keeps talking, but I can't make out the words.

4338327950288419716939937510582O9 …

The numbers get louder. Bigger. And brighter.

749445923O7816406286208998628O348253421170 …

I stand up. All the way up. I only meant to come up an inch. I have no control over me. The kid next to me—his name is Levi, according to the paper on his desk—turns his head real quick like I've scared him.

I sit again.

I stand again.

I sit. Finally. My face heats up like I have the worst case of sunburn. No one says anything, but I'm in the 2nd row, and I know the 18 kids who are not in the front row all noticed my weirdness. Windy is in the front and misses it all, which is a relief because she would have said something or asked, *What are you doing?*

Announcements come over the classroom speaker. The principal welcomes us all to another great school year. While he reads an inspirational quote, I slip an individually wrapped Clorox wipe from my backpack and clean my desk.

Levi watches me with his mouth open. He has dark eyes (that I wish would stop looking at me), brown skin, and black curly hair that's thick on top of his head and shaved to almost nothing on the sides. He stares as if he's never seen anyone clean before. It's not like I'm doing a magic trick or a dangerous science experiment. When I finish wiping the top, I show him the cloth. It's black with grime.

He wrinkles his face in disgust. I'm not sure whether the look is for the dirt or for me.

I slip the dirty wipe into a sandwich bag to throw away later. I'll probably collect 15 to 20 wipes during the day.

Homeroom lasts for 10 minutes. Afterward, we stay in our seats, and Mr. Stoker starts his class. I'm disappointed because he spends his 50 minutes going over rules and policy. I wanted to hear him talk about math, even if it was only addition.

When the bell rings, I get up slowly. I don't want to bump into kids in the doorway.

"What do you have next?" Windy asks.

"Room 304. Spanish." I've already finished 6 semesters of high school Spanish online. I can't speak it well, but I'm great at memorizing words.

"I have technology. Then language arts 3rd. You do, too, right? We should have all our core classes together. That's how it works."

"Yeah." I nod.

"Well, then I'll see you in 50 minutes."

If I survive that long.

I've watched enough TV to know that cafeterias are rooms of torture and humiliation in both schools and prisons. But East Hamlin Middle is different from what I'd imagined. We don't walk to lunch on our own. We go to 4th period, which for me is science. Then Ms. Bryson marches us to the cafeteria in a quiet single-file line. There's no picking seats around the room. The entire class is forced to sit together at a giant table like we're a big happy family.

"Take any empty seat," Ms. Bryson says. "You have 25 minutes. That's it."

The stools are attached to the tables. We can't move our seats closer to the table or farther from our classmates.

"Be right back. Save me a seat," Windy says. She joins the end of the food line.

I take an empty stool 1 seat away from Levi. I sit, stand, sit, stand, sit. He groans.

"Is this seat taken?" I ask. I really don't want to start over.

"Looks like you took it 3 times already."

The table reeks of cleaning stuff. I still don't trust it. I take out my 5th wipe of the day.

"Hey, cleaning lady," a girl farther down the table calls out. "Will you wipe my spot, too?"

I offer her an extra individually wrapped Clorox wipe. This makes her and the girls on each side of her fall over laughing.

"You're such a freak." She rolls her eyes.

I use my wipe. The dirt and germs bother me more than the nasty comments.

"You're really good at that," the girl says. "Do you do toilets, too?"

I try to avoid public restrooms except in emergencies, but if I do need to go, I disinfect the toilet seat. Then I put down a layer of toilet paper for protection. I also clean the faucet handles and the paper-towel dispenser. And then I wash my hands for a minimum of 2 minutes in the hottest water available. In my opinion, it's never hot enough. But I don't explain any of this to the girl. I'm pretty sure she doesn't want me to answer her question.

Levi grabs the used wipe out of my hand. He holds it up to show the girl and her friends.

"How do you like this, Maddie?"

She wrinkles her lips and scrunches her nose. "This place is so disgusting." Then she stands up. "Let's move."

"Sit down," Ms. Bryson barks from the staff table next to ours. "Lunch isn't over."

"We need to move." Maddie says we, but she's the only 1 who stood up.

"Sit! Down!"

Maddie slowly sinks back into her seat. Her eyes narrow at me. Suddenly, she stands back up like something pinched her butt. The entire class turns her direction. It's quiet for the 1st time. Maddie slowly sits again.

I know what's coming.

Please don't.

She stands again. Sits. Stands. Everyone laughs.

"Enough!" Ms. Bryson yells. Her mouth is full of salad, and her voice doesn't have the force she probably intended.

"Sorry, I'm done," Maddie says sweetly.

I use hand sanitizer (approximately 3 times the recommended amount) and then focus on my lunch. Nana packed me a ham sandwich on white bread, a bag of plain potato chips, a peanut butter granola bar, and a fruit punch juice box. I wonder what would be the easiest to choke on.

"That was a good impression, Maddie," a boy at the end of the table says over the laughing. "Y'all even look alike."

"Who?" Maddie shrieks.

"You and the cleaning lady."

"Ick! No! Way!" Maddie says it like she's being compared to a llama. I don't like it, either. But I'm not making gagging noises. We both have long brown hair pulled into a braid. But mine falls halfway down my back, the style similar to what I wore in elementary school. Maddie's is a trendy side braid pulled over her right shoulder. We have white skin and brown eyes. At least I think her eyes are brown. I haven't looked at her long enough to know for certain. And thanks to the school's SMOD policy, we're dressed like twins in white polo shirts and navy-blue shorts (like the number 7).

I play with my lightning-bolt necklace and make a wish. *Make me invisible. Make this all go away.* But Uncle Paul said the charm was lucky, not magical.

Nana has included a note on my napkin: *It won't kill you to smile.* I'm starting to think Nana never went to middle school.

Windy sits down next to me. "What did I miss?"

"Nothing." I don't have the energy to tell her.

"I'm starving, but I'm not sure any of this is actually food," she says. Her tray has yellowy chicken strips (the color of the number 102), an apple, mashed potatoes, and chocolate milk.

Windy takes a bite of chicken, chews twice, and then starts talking.

"So, Lucy," she says, "tell us your story."

"There's nothing to tell. Nothing interesting, anyway." I take a drink from my juice box.

"You're new. New is always interesting."

"Not this time."

"Fine, I get it," Windy says. "You're shy. Why don't I tell you something about everyone else, and then you'll feel more comfortable."

"You don't have to." I look at the clock. We still have 17 minutes left of this torture called lunch.

"Don't worry. I'll tell you something good and not so good. That's the only right way to do it."

"The right way is to not talk about people at all," Levi says, staring at his carrot sticks.

"Oh, look," Windy says. "A volunteer. That's Levi Boyd. He has 2 moms—"

"Hey!"

"That's your good trait. I've met his moms. I volunteered with them at a soup kitchen last Thanksgiving. They're awesome people." Windy taps her heart. "Now his flaws. Do I really need to pick just 1?"

"Stop talking." Levi pulls the hood of his East Hamlin sweatshirt over his head, covering his curly black hair.

"Levi thinks he's part of the paparazzi. He's always taking pictures, and not on his phone. It's weird." She pauses like she's waiting for Levi to fire back. But he ignores her. No one else seems to be paying any attention to Windy and me, either. Maybe the necklace *is* magical.

"Moving on. That's Lincoln Chandler," Windy continues. Her voice is softer. "He's an awesome soccer player and he has a severe Brazil nut allergy. Do you have any Brazil nuts in your lunch? Because they could literally kill him."

I shake my head and hold up my granola bar. "It's peanut butter."

The rest of Windy's lunch lies untouched as she goes around the table, giving me the details about everyone. They all start to blend together. Good at baseball, spelling, musical theater, drawing manga. She doesn't mention anyone being good at math. As for the negatives, she talks a lot about allergies and weird hobbies, like the kid who collects movie ticket stubs. And not just for movies he's gone to.

"He'll buy your used tickets for a quarter," she says.

"He hasn't done that since 4th grade," Levi says.

"Whatever. Where was I?" Windy pauses. There are only 2 people she hasn't summed up yet: herself and Maddie, the girl who called me the cleaning lady. "I guess that leaves me."

"Let me," Levi jumps in. "Windy Sitton loves a charity case." His brown eyes focus on mine for a second, and it feels like a warning. "Lives for it."

She smiles. "True. I like to think I'm making a difference in the world."

"Windy Sitton likes musicals, though she can't sing."

"True, too."

"She's also bossy and nosy and has an opinion about everything." He counts the traits on his fingers.

"True and true and true. I'm a born leader. I speak my mind. And it's not like I'm reading people's diaries or breaking into lockers. I'm observant. Your turn, Lucy." She shovels a spoonful of mashed potatoes into her mouth.

"What about her?" I nod toward Maddie. I don't really want to know. I'm stalling.

Windy swallows. "That's Maddie Thornton. She does gymnastics and dance. And she's a really good singer. She sang the national anthem at a professional baseball game last year."

"It was minor league," Levi adds. "And she got the words wrong."

Windy continues like Levi didn't say anything. "Maddie and I were best friends in 5th grade, and our moms have known each other forever. She's also wicked smart."

"You mean just plain wicked," Levi mumbles.

"She's not that bad," Windy says. "Now it's definitely

your turn, Lucy, unless you want me to talk about the teachers, too. Ms. Fleming went through a nasty divorce over the summer."

"Okay. Um…"

"Tell us something good 1st." She says *us*, but no one else is listening, except maybe Levi.

"I'm good at math."

"Okay." She seems disappointed.

"You already know my … um … routine."

"The sitting thing?" she asks.

"Yeah." She missed it in math class but got to witness it in language arts and twice in science.

She laughs. "Maybe you really aren't interesting."

"Told you. I'm mostly ordinary." At least that's what I want everyone to think. Lightning Girl, your ordinary, everyday savant cleaning lady.

7

Nana is waiting when I get off the bus. She's the only adult around. I'd be embarrassed if I weren't so relieved to be done with my 1st day.

I tap my toe 3 times as she wraps me in a hug.

"How was it?" Judging by her huge smile, I'd say she's expecting to hear good news.

"If I tell you it was torture, that everyone thinks I'm a freak, that I probably caught a disease from accidentally touching the bus's handrail, that the teachers act like prison guards, and that I hated all 400 minutes of it, will you still make me go back?"

"Yes."

I shrug. "Then it was fine." I walk toward our building.

"Lucy." Nana follows me. "And what do you know about prison guards? That's not a fair comparison."

"This whole thing isn't fair."

"You think you're the 1st kid who doesn't want to go to school? Please." Nana walks ahead of me. She opens the door so I don't have to touch it.

It's only 1 year, I repeat to myself. I can suffer through a year of middle school. But it still seems like a waste. I should be dedicating my life to solving the unsolvable problems of mathematics, like the Riemann hypothesis or the Hodge conjecture.

"Your uncle wants you to call him," Nana says as she turns on the TV. "He wants to hear all about your big day. Try not to complain too much."

I use my new cell phone. Nana, Uncle Paul, and our neighbor Mrs. Chapman are the only people whose numbers are programmed into it. Not that I need the phone numbers saved. They're all locked in my brain.

"Hey, genius," Uncle Paul answers. "How was—" The phone call breaks in and out, but I know what he's asking.

"It was the absolute worst." I say this loud enough for Nana to hear. I want her to know I need more than her prayers. I need out of that school.

"Middle school is supposed to be the worst. It's like a giant hazing for adulthood. We all gotta go through it."

"No, we don't."

"Lucy. Come on. You can do this. You're—" The line cuts out again.

"I don't belong there." I twist my lightning-bolt necklace.

"Have you ever heard the saying 'Fake it till you make it'?" he asks.

"I don't know. Maybe."

"It means you gotta act like you belong or act like you can do something, and eventually you'll be able to."

"That doesn't make any sense."

He gives an exaggerated sigh. "Go to school tomorrow with a big smile on your face and act like you belong there."

Why do all adults think smiling is the answer?

"I do belong there, but only according to my age and the law."

"That's right. And act like you belong at the popular lunch table and on the chess or basketball team or whatever extracurricular you want to do. Eventually, you'll go from faking it to making it. It's all about confidence. Are you writing this down?"

"No."

"You should be. I'm basically giving you the secret to life, kiddo. No charge."

"Gee, thanks."

"Hey, I gotta go. Call me later if you need more advice.

And at some point, we need to talk about boys. I've got a lot to say on the subject. Okay? I love you, genius."

"Love you, too." I put my phone away and grab a box of Oreos from the cabinet.

"What did Uncle Paul have to say?" Nana asks from the living room.

"He told me to be fake." I shove a cookie into my mouth.

"That's horrible. You need to be yourself, Lucy. Give it time."

"I'm giving it 1 year. That was the deal." I take another cookie and get some milk from the fridge. We don't have any real homework today. Nana needs to sign a few papers. That's all. I kind of wanted math homework. That would have been something fun to do. Maybe other kids at other schools are luckier than I am and actually got assigned math problems.

I go to my room and log on to my favorite site, MathWhiz. I've been tagged in 14 forum questions.

LightningGirl, help!

I love you, LightningGirl.

LG, if you can solve this freakin' problem, I'm going to marry you and we'll make little lightning babies.

Okay, that last 1 is super creepy.

Maddie may rule at East Hamlin. Windy might know everything about everyone. But here, I'm queen.

Nana goes to work at Cracker Barrel. And I stay on

the computer until 10:00 p.m., solving people's problems and chatting with SquareHead314.

SquareHead314: You were missed today.

LightningGirl: I had class

SquareHead314: What are you teaching?

Is it lying if I don't correct him?

LightningGirl: It's only an intro class. Nothing exciting.

SquareHead314: Glad you could still make time for us.

LightningGirl: Trust me, I'd rather be here

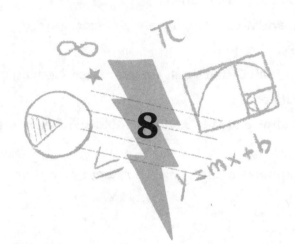

8

I won't admit it to anyone, but I'm looking forward to math class. I'm sure Mr. Stoker will spend the year covering topics I mastered when I was 8. But to me, it's like hearing a favorite band sing an old song or re-watching a favorite episode of *Supernatural*.

Math class doesn't start right away, because we are assigned our lockers during 1st period. Mr. Stoker hands us each a sheet with our locations and combinations. My combo is 48–9–27. All divisible by 3. Multiplied to-gether they equal 11,664, and that number has a perfect square root, 108!

My locker number isn't nearly as impressive. 250B. The *B* means that it's on the bottom, and it's directly below Maddie's—250A. It may be the worst location in the school. Windy's locker is in a different section, on the other side of the door to room 213.

Levi is sort of a neighbor. His locker is 252B. He doesn't say anything as he throws some books in, slams the door closed, and locks it. Maddie takes her time placing binders and hanging a mirror. I wait for her to finish before disinfecting my lock.

I *want* to clean my locker quickly. I *want* to get back to math class. I open another wipe. I'm going to need at least 3 more. Crumbs and pencil shavings cover the bottom, and it smells like wet shoes. I clean the sides, the back, and the hooks. It's the locker's floor that's a problem. Each pass of the cloth collects grime, debris, and even hair.

"1 more minute," Mr. Stoker warns.

Only 2 other girls are still in the hallway. I open another wipe. 5 wrappers lie on the ground. If I use any more now, I won't have enough for the rest of the day. I scrub until the cloth rips. My locker is still not sanitized.

My neck is hot. I can hear blood rushing through my ears. The digits of pi tick through my brain.

3.141592653 . . .

I tap my toe 3 times to make the numbers fade away. Maybe I can get some paper towels and spray from a janitor.

"Back to your seats, please," Mr. Stoker says.

The other girls slam their doors closed. I do, too. Without putting anything inside my locker. I can't.

"May I use the bathroom?" I ask as the others go back into the classroom.

"Lucy, it's time to . . ." He stares at the used wipes and wrappers in my hands. "Make it quick."

In the girls' room, I throw away the garbage and quickly wash my hands using 3 squirts of soap. On the way back to class, I use 3 pumps of hand sanitizer.

Mr. Stoker is at the front of the room, erasing the whiteboard. I haven't missed anything. Was he waiting for me?

I sit, stand, sit, stand, sit in my seat. Someone clears a throat. Someone else sighs. Maybe they're disgusted by me. Or maybe those are just classroom noises.

I take out my mechanical pencil. Mr. Stoker finally turns around, ready to begin. My mind floods with the possibilities. It could be something beautifully simple. Even finding the area of a circle (area = πr^2) would be interesting. I love any formula that requires pi. If I ever got a tattoo, it would be π.

I expect him to pick up 1 of the dry erase markers that sit on the ledge. He doesn't. Maybe he's going to explain a theory using simple, clear terms. Instead, he walks to his desk and grabs a pile of papers.

"This is not a test," he says.

Still, most of the class groans on cue.

"This is an assessment," Mr. Stoker continues. "To see where you are and where the class is as a whole. I'll use it to determine where we need to start."

He gives the 1st person in each row a few sheets to pass back.

"Does it count for a grade?" a boy behind me asks.

"No. But you should still do your best. You learned some of this stuff in 6th grade, and some of it you probably have not been taught."

I raise my hand, slowly and carefully, like I'm putting my arm inside a bees' nest.

"Lucy?"

I suddenly realize how weird my question is, and I try to think of another instead. I can't, so I just say what's on my mind.

"If we finish quickly, will you have time to start our 1st lesson?"

There's a distinct giggle. Maddie.

"Let's focus on the assessment today. I'd like everyone to take their time. If you're done early, check it over."

The not-a-test sits on my desk. On the front page are 10 questions. I've already answered them all in my head.

41

15

2

$x = y^2$

1, −1

13

6

True

True

False

I turn to the 2nd page. The answers fly into my head in a swirl of colorful number shapes. In less than 2 minutes, I'm done. At least in my weirdly wired brain. I haven't written anything yet. I look around the room. Heads are down. Pencils are moving. Levi's desk is the closest. He's only written his name and some calculations under the 1st problem. He's got the answer wrong.

Suddenly, Levi turns and looks at me. I drop my head like he caught me watching him get dressed. I take my hair out of my headband and try to hide my face. I can't see him, but somehow I still feel his eyes on me.

Mr. Stoker turns on a small speaker. Classical music that reminds me of a jewelry-store commercial fills the room.

"Relax, everyone," he says. "Just do your best."

I already know my best is going to be the class's best. I might even be better than Mr. Stoker. Probably. It's not his fault.

I glance again at Levi's paper. He wrote 7 as the answer to question number 1. But he got his order of operations wrong. He needed to square before adding.

The answer is 41.

I write down 7.

I can't hide my need to sit-stand or tap my toe 3 times, or my obsession with de-germing any and all surfaces. But I can hide my superpower. They don't need to know. I'm not hurting anyone. I can fake it till I make it. I can fake being normal, and eventually I will be.

Maybe.

Slowly, I fill in the rest of the answers. I make 3 more mistakes. If this were for a grade, I'd get an 82, or a B. I plan on getting an A in the class. I mean, I don't want to ruin my chances of getting into college next year.

Nana wants 1 year, 1 friend, 1 book, and 1 activity. I calculate this will be easier to achieve without being a freaky genius. I can be *normal* smart. It's only middle school. This is about survival.

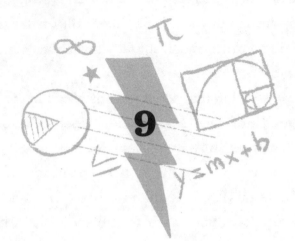

Nana's cell phone rings at 6:42, as we are cleaning up from dinner. I can tell from her face that she doesn't recognize the number on the ID.

"Hello?"

I carry our cups to the sink.

"This is she." Nana looks at me and raises an eyebrow.

Usually, I like to wash the dishes. I use the hottest water to rinse away all the food and microbes. But tonight, I have the urge to run to my room. I turn. I'm too slow. Nana grabs my shoulder.

"Well, can she take it over?" She pauses for an answer that I can't hear. "I see." Pause. "Certainly." Pause.

"Thanks for calling. Good-bye." She puts the phone down on the counter.

"Wrong number?" I joke.

"That was your math teacher. He said you got a 0 on today's test."

"What!" It wasn't even a test. It was an assessment.

"Lucy, what's going on?"

My face feels hot. "I did not get a 0."

"It's what he said." Nana threw up her hands. "Is this a cry for help, Lucy? Are you trying to prove some point? Because I don't get it. Your old grandmother isn't as smart as you. Tell me what's going on."

"I did not get a 0!" I shout. "I got an 82."

"Lower your voice. Mrs. Chapman is going to hear you yelling through the walls." Nana reaches for me, but I step back. "Tell me what's going on."

I want to go to my room, but I know she'll follow me, and the lock on the door doesn't work.

"I got a few answers wrong on purpose. I didn't want to stick out." *Any more than I already do.* "I promise I didn't get a 0. He made a mistake."

"You took a dive on a math test? That's out of character."

"An 82 isn't exactly a dive. And it's not a secret cry for help. I don't want to go to that school. You know that, Nana. But if I have to be there, I don't want to be the savant or the genius." I don't want to be the cleaning lady, either.

"Suit yourself. At least you're developing some acting skills. In case you decide you don't want to devote your whole life to math." She wiggles her eyebrows at me.

"And you should be a comedian." I wiggle my eyebrows back.

"Maybe I will." She turns to the sink. "Your teacher wants you to stay after school tomorrow. I'll pick you up at 3."

"Fine." I go to my room and log on to MathWhiz. My life is still homework-free. I help in the calculus forum for 30 minutes, and then I check out the trigonometry page. SquareHead314 has already answered the most interesting questions. I send him/her a message.

LightningGirl: you didn't leave anything fun for me

SquareHead314: It's the beginning of the school year.

SquareHead314: Not a lot of fun happening yet.

LightningGirl: true

SquareHead314: If you're bored . . .

SquareHead314: why don't you set up tomorrow's problem of the day?

SquareHead314 and HipHypotenuse put up ridiculously easy math problems on the forums every day. Usually something like, "Susie and Sally are going to a brunch with 8 other people. What's the probability they will sit next to each other?"

LightningGirl: OK

SquareHead314: But don't make it too hard this time. No one got your last 1.

LightningGirl: you did

SquareHead314: Aim a little lower.

LightningGirl: that's my new motto

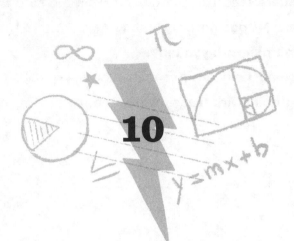

Math mystery solved: I got every answer "wrong" on my math assessment because I did not show my calculations. I thought I was careful, but I failed to read the 1st line of instructions: *Show all work.*

I'm not the only 1 who screwed up. Levi has to stay after school with me.

Mr. Stoker asks us both to sit in the front row. I sit, stand, sit, stand, sit at Windy's desk. I don't wipe it down, but I don't touch it, either.

Mr. Stoker pulls his wooden stool over and half sits on it. "Mathematics is not only about getting the correct answer. It's about being on the road to the correct answer.

Knowing the path can be just as important as knowing the solution."

I completely disagree but stay quiet. Math is about right answers and proving the right answer. I love mathematic proofs, but I don't think we'll get into them in 7th grade.

"If you take each problem a step at a time," he continues, "you'll grow the answer organically. The process will take root in your brain. This is true learning." He folds his hands and closes his eyes like he's meditating.

"I'll show my work from now on," I say, staring at the non-clean desk.

Out of the corner of my eye, I see Levi nod.

"Good. But that's not the only issue here. You had similar answers. Only 2 were actually different, and considering that most of your incorrect answers were identical, you can understand why I needed to speak with you."

What?

He holds up the tests. Levi wrote down the same answers as I did for 8 of the 10 questions on the 1st page. Sure, I'd copied the wrong answer for question number 1. Now I realize how stupid that was. Major miscalculation.

Mr. Stoker stays very calm, which makes me both nervous and sad. I've already decided he's my favorite teacher. He did a nice job today reviewing how to add, subtract, multiply, and divide exponents. Not hard concepts, but he got really excited, and he gave us M&M's.

"So who borrowed answers from whom and why?" he asks. "This was not for a grade. The motive for cheating on the 2nd day of school is unclear to me, especially when we'd reviewed the class policy and school honor code the day before. This is serious."

I want to shout, *Levi copied! Levi cheated!* Because it's mostly true. He did *most* of the cheating. Instead, I look over at him, hoping that he'll confess and we can leave. He keeps his chin down and his arms crossed over his chest. He looks like he's asleep.

"Middle school is tough. There's a lot of pressure coming at you from every angle. I think we can work this out and avoid any severe punishment. I'm not condoning cheating. And if it happens again, I will use the highest penalty in my power."

I don't know what the highest penalty is.

"So, does anyone want to confess?"

I watch 15 seconds tick by on the clock. Plenty of time for Levi to be brave and own up.

He doesn't.

"I didn't cheat," I whisper.

Levi looks up. "I didn't cheat." He says it louder than I did.

"What? Yes, you did." I'm not whispering anymore.

Mr. Stoker takes a deep breath. "I'm going to step into the hall so you can talk for a minute." He grabs a water bottle off his desk and leaves us alone.

"Why are you doing this?" I ask as soon as Mr. Stoker closes the door.

Levi shrugs.

"You're the 1 who cheated."

"I know."

"Tell him," I say. "You won't get in trouble."

"You believe him?" Levi looks at me for the 1st time. "He's setting us up. It's a trap."

"It's not a trap." Not that I would know what a teacher's trap would look like.

Levi shrugs. "If we both stay quiet, what can he do?"

I don't want to think about what he can do. Maybe I'll get kicked out of middle school in my 1st week.

Maybe that isn't a bad thing.

Then Levi says, "You didn't cover your answers. You put them right out where I could see them. And when you were done, you didn't even turn the test over on your desk. I thought you were sharing."

"What? Why would I share?" I definitely wasn't sharing. I have a pain in my head thinking this could all have been avoided if I'd flipped my paper over.

"And I thought you were *good* at math." He doesn't say this like it's a compliment.

"Why would you think that?" I don't like touching people, not even shaking hands, but I want to slap Levi at this moment. I can't believe I'm having violent thoughts. Middle school is turning me into a monster.

"You said it at lunch the 1st day."

"I didn't mean ... whatever. Please, tell him the truth." Math class is the only not-awful part of my day. If Mr. Stoker thinks I'm a cheat, it could ruin those 50 minutes.

Levi leans over and pulls something from his backpack. It's a camera. He aims it at me and takes a picture. I throw my hands over my face a second too late.

"What are you doing? Don't take my picture."

"It's for my *angry* collection."

What? "Stop."

He puts the camera back, but not before taking another picture of me, with my mouth hanging open.

"What's with the lightning bolt?" He points at my necklace. "Is it a Harry Potter thing?"

Mr. Stoker knocks loudly and opens the door.

"Just tell him you cheated," I whisper-yell at Levi.

"No."

"Why?"

He doesn't get a chance to answer. Mr. Stoker stands in front of us with his hands on his hips and his foot tapping.

"So?" That's all he says.

"I didn't cheat," Levi says superquick.

"I didn't cheat, either." I ball my hands into fists. *Why did I say* either?

For the next 15 minutes, Mr. Stoker lectures us on being honest and working hard and having principles.

But Levi and I never confess. Not that I have anything to confess to—other than borrowing 1 wrong answer.

When we are finally allowed to leave, Levi and I walk out together. I'm mad. The only thing I've ever plotted before is graph points. But now I'm plotting revenge.

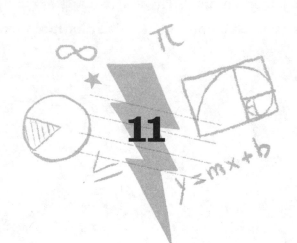

My revenge tactic has mostly been not talking to Levi for the last 45 hours. But I'm not sure he noticed, so I'm extending it to at least a week. He sits to my left during lunch, keeping his head down like his cheese sandwich is the most interesting thing in the room. Maybe the silent treatment isn't the right way to get back at Levi.

I twist in my seat to face Windy and put my back toward Levi. I wonder if he notices my rudeness. Windy does most of the talking, here at lunch and on the bus. I'm learning a lot about the similarities between the musicals *Les Misérables* and *Hamilton*.

"You can listen to them online. I know you'll love

them," she says between spoonfuls of yogurt. "So, will you listen to them?"

"Sure."

"Awesome. I'll listen with you. Can I come over to your house today?" Windy asks. "I'll text my mom later, but I'm sure it's okay."

I close my eyes and picture our apartment and my room. Is there anything that might give away my secret? My walls are decorated with images of the Fibonacci spiral in nature: flower petals, pinecones, nautilus shells, far-off galaxies. But Windy would probably assume I love nature, not numbers. I have a collection of math and engineering textbooks on the top shelf of my desk. Nana buys them at garage sales, and most were printed in the 1950s and '60s. They'd be harder to explain.

"I guess, but I don't have a house. We live in an apartment." I tug on my lightning-bolt necklace. Part of me is hoping that this is not okay and she won't be able to come over.

"Cool." She puts her arm out like she's going to hug me or high-five me, and I jump back in my seat. My elbow knocks into something. I turn to see Levi's chocolate milk puddling across the table.

He groans.

"I'm sorry," I mumble. His sandwich and chips are already soggy. I drop 4 Clorox wipes onto the table and struggle to open a 5th individual packet. This cuts into my daily supply, but I still have enough for the rest of my classes.

Other kids, including Maddie and Jennifer, hand Levi their napkins. I do the same.

Levi picks up his ruined lunch and carries it to the garbage can. Other kids move their trays away from the puddle. Levi comes back with a roll of paper towels to mop up the mess. My mess.

Serves you right for cheating. I only say this in my head, and it doesn't make me feel any better.

"Sorry," I whisper again.

"It was an accident," Levi replies. The brown paper towels aren't exactly superabsorbent. He needs half a roll to soak up the milk.

When the table is finally clean, Levi sits down. Then he pretends to bite into an invisible sandwich. The kid across from him laughs. Then Levi peels an invisible banana and pretends to eat it. More kids are laughing.

"Enough of the mime act," Maddie says, but not in a mean way. She's laughing, too. Then she reaches into the small handbag that she carries cross-body.

"Here!" She holds out a couple of $1 bills to Levi. "Go buy some more chips or an ice cream."

Levi looks at the money. "No thanks."

"I'll take it," another kid says.

"No," Maddie says. She shoves the bills into Levi's

hand. "Just take it." Then she turns to Jasmine, who is on the other side of her.

Levi stares at the money for a second, then shrugs and walks to the food line. A minute later, he's back with Doritos and more chocolate milk. When he walks past Maddie, he says a quiet thank-you. He doesn't even look my direction.

∞

Windy follows me off the bus and to my apartment. As she'd predicted, her mom agreed to the visit. I offer Windy a squirt of hand sanitizer when we get inside. Nana isn't home. She's working the day shift at Cracker Barrel.

"Do you want a snack?" I ask as I clean the kitchen table with a Clorox wipe.

"Yes. Please tell me you have something other than fruit or nonfat yogurt. That's all we have at home."

"We've got Twizzlers."

"Yes!"

I move a box of oatmeal and a carton of bread crumbs to get to the candy stash. Nana and I both know where the candy is hidden. I'm not sure who we are hiding it from. Robbers or the landlord, I guess.

I offer Windy the open bag. She takes 3. I bite off the end of a Twizzler. And then I sit, stand, sit, stand, sit at the kitchen table. It's easier to keep secrets if we stay out of my room.

"I don't get why you do that," Windy says through a mouthful. She takes a seat next to me.

I shrug. "I don't know, either."

"Then just stop."

"I can't."

"It's an OCD thing, right? Obsessive-compulsive disorder."

"Yeah. I guess." Nana took me to a psychologist 3 years ago. Dr. Walsh set up a treatment plan and said that with some mild medication and "gradual exposure to your triggers," we could control my OCD. I asked her if that meant the digits of pi would go away. She answered, "Yes, with some work." And with that, I refused to go back. I wouldn't mind losing my sit-stand routine or not worrying about germs. But no one was taking away pi.

"I have an aunt with OCD," Windy says. "She has to touch both sides of the doorframe like 10 times before she can walk through the door. She says if she doesn't touch it, something horrible will happen to her kids." She explains her aunt like she's giving me the instructions for a board game.

"It's not exactly like that for me." I bite off another piece of candy.

"Then, what's it like?"

"If I don't do my routine ... if I don't sit-stand 3 times, or I don't tap my toe 3 times when I stop walking, stuff messes with my head."

"What kind of stuff? Demons?" She opens her eyes wide.

"No. Just numbers." I hold open the bag of Twizzlers. She takes another 3. I wonder if she's taking 3 at a time on purpose.

"Thanks."

"This string of numbers takes over my brain if I don't follow my pattern. It's like an alien invasion in my head. The digits are loud and bright, and I can't do anything else. I can't even think about anything else, because they block everything." I don't tell her the numbers are digits of pi. That's an unnecessary detail.

"That's weird, but at least you have a way to stop it. You have the secret antidote or the weapon that stops the aliens. Sit 3 times or tap your foot 3 times and you're fine."

"Yep. My magic formula that freaks people out."

"Imagine if you couldn't stop the number invasion. That would be worse."

"I guess that's true."

We finish the 1-pound bag of Twizzlers. I grab 2 Sprites and a sleeve of Chips Ahoy! cookies, and we go into the living room to watch TV. Windy seems to have forgotten she wanted me to listen to Broadway musicals this afternoon, and I'm not going to remind her.

"You have endless supplies of sugar here. I may never leave," Windy says.

I let Windy have the remote. She flips channels until she comes to a commercial.

"Oooh, oooh," she grunts at the TV. Cookie crumbs fly from her mouth.

"What's wrong?" I know she's not choking, because she's making too much noise.

She points at the screen. It's a commercial for Rocky Mountain Lodge. I've seen it before, and it's not that exciting. A family enjoys a day of water rides, followed by a meal and a hug from a raccoon mascot, and then the kids are tucked into bed by very happy parents.

"My mom says I can have my birthday party there," Windy says when the commercial is over.

"Cool."

She doesn't seem impressed by my reaction. "Have you ever been?"

"No."

"It's going to be awesome." She holds out her hands like awesome can be measured as a distance. "We're going to stay overnight in a suite, and we're going to go on every ride. That's assuming I get all A's 1st quarter. But that shouldn't be a problem."

"When's your birthday?" I ask.

"November 10th."

"That's not for 71 days."

Windy opens her mouth dramatically like a cartoon character. "What the what?"

"I think it's 71 days." I laugh and rub my palms on my khaki shorts.

Windy pulls out her cell phone. She taps the screen. Then she shrugs. "You're right."

"I'm good with dates. It's a game I play with my grandmother. We call it countdown. It's really not hard. We know how many days are in each month. Right?"

"I guess."

We watch TV and finish our snack. I actually like having Windy over, but I'm dying to know if anyone solved my epic problem in the math forums. I wrote it so that it seemed supersimple, but there was a twist. I bet 90 percent of people miss it.

"I'll be right back." I get up. Windy doesn't ask me where I'm going. She's focused on a show about children's working conditions in Bangladesh.

I boot up the computer and log on to MathWhiz. 41 people have tried to solve my problem. I scroll through the solutions. *Wrong. Wrong. Wrong.*

But then I see it. The right answer. It was posted by MathMaster.

I write in the comments: *Awesome. You got it.* I don't admit that part of me is disappointed that the 4th person figured it out. The next 37 posts are all arguments about whether MathMaster was right.

"Lucy!" Windy calls from the living room. "My sister is here."

"Coming." I turn off the computer, saying good-bye to my e-friends, and go back to the actual human in my living room. Not that my online buddies aren't *actually humans.*

"I gotta go." She walks over and gives me a 1-armed hug around the shoulders. I don't move. I don't breathe. I don't approve. "Next time, you can come to my house. But you'll have to smuggle in the good food."

Nana told me to make 1 friend. And I guess I have. She may be using me for a sugar rush, but that's okay.

12

On Tuesday, all 7th graders have to miss part of 1st period for an assembly. My 1st-period class is math, the only part of my day that I like. I would rather have the assembly during language arts or gym or lunch. But no one asked me.

Mr. Stoker hands back our homework—I got a 92, on purpose—and says to the class, "Let's go, ladies and gentlemen. Dr. Cobb doesn't like to wait."

Levi and I stand up at the same time. I want to say, *Done any cheating lately?* But then I see his homework grade. He got a 45. I decide to continue giving him the silent treatment.

Our class sits in the 4th and 5th rows of the auditorium. I'm able to sit—doing my usual 3rd-time's-a-charm routine—without touching the armrest, so I don't need my Clorox wipes. Windy is on my left. Maddie is supposed to take the seat to my right, but she leaves it empty and takes the next chair over. This makes Mr. Stoker upset.

"Move all the way over, Maddie." He points to the empty seat next to me.

She does what he says. And then the 11 kids to her right have to slide over so that no seat is left empty.

Mr. Stoker smiles at me like he's done me a favor. He hasn't.

"Don't look at me. Don't breathe on me," Maddie whispers. We both lean in opposite directions.

After all the classes arrive, the principal gets on the stage.

"Good morning, East Hamlin Cougars," Dr. Cobb begins.

Some people mumble a reply of *Good morning*—mostly the teachers.

"By all accounts, we seem to be off to a great school year. Teachers are already handing out piles of homework, and the cafeteria is serving veggie sloppy joes. It makes a principal proud." He pauses, maybe waiting for a laugh. "But let's be serious. It's now time to lay a strong foundation for your education and your future. At East

Hamlin Middle, we expect our students to flourish not only in the classroom but also in the community.

"This year, like every year, you will be required to complete a service project. Last year, your projects were class-wide. As 7th graders, you will work in teams of 3 or 4 students to identify a need in your community and a solution. This is your chance to make a difference. You can change the world for the better."

Dr. Cobb uses his hands a lot when he talks. He seems to be counting off items on his fingers, but I can't imagine what.

"Mrs. Jensen runs the program and will give you more information." Dr. Cobb claps as Mrs. Jensen steps forward. The students clap, too—sort of.

The screen at the back of the stage flitters with color. A PowerPoint presentation pops onto it. I count the words before I read them (9 words, 50 letters, 1 colon): COUGARS CARE PROJECTS: MAKING A DIFFERENCE IN OUR COMMUNITY.

"I know what you're thinking," Mrs. Jensen says to us—a statement I always find weird because I'm never able to guess what another person is thinking. And she claims to know what an entire 7th-grade class is thinking. "You're asking yourself, how can I make a difference? I'm only 12 or 13 years old. I can't drive. I don't have any money. I have homework and soccer and dance. How can I help my community?"

That wasn't what I was thinking. I was calculating the number of hours left in the school year. 1,160.

"Here are some of the projects that 7th graders—students the same as you—have tackled over the past few years." She waves at the screen with 1 hand and uses her other hand to press a button on a laptop that sits on the podium.

We watch a video that profiles different projects. The 1st shows 3 girls in matching shirts bringing Legos to a local children's hospital. The next features 4 boys who collect old sports equipment to send to Kenya. I never really thought of Kenya as part of my community, but 1 of the boys says because of technology, we have to think of our community on a global scale. The last group is 2 girls and a boy. They organize a day where people help clean Liberty Park. It actually seems like the most work out of the 3 projects. They get sweaty and dirty, and it doesn't look like much fun.

When the video finishes, Mrs. Jensen claps. "And that is only a sample of the great accomplishments by our students in the past few years. And now it's your turn. When you return to 1st period, you will receive a packet with all the details. There are several deadlines along the way. The 1st is next Friday. By then, you'll need to have formed a team of 3 or 4 students and selected a teacher mentor to help you through this project. And by the end of the month, your group will identify a situation in our community that can use your help."

Mrs. Jensen goes on about some of the other rules. The projects can't be political. Like no handing out flyers for people running for president. We also aren't allowed to raise money for a cause. We can collect stuff but not cash. And there are rules about religion, too, but they are even more unclear.

Windy grabs my arm when Mrs. Jensen finishes.

"We'll be a team, right?"

"Sure," I say. "But we need another person."

"I'll find someone. No problem. Then we're going to change the world." She says it like she believes it.

"Great." I want to be excited with her. But I don't think we'll even be able to find someone willing to work with us—willing to work with *me*. And changing the world is a tall order for someone who is just trying to survive each day.

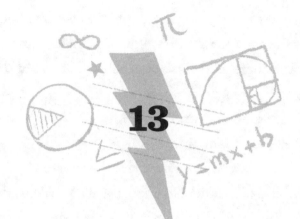

13

There's no need to hide my genius in language arts class because I'm not a genius in language arts class. I'm a decent reader and an okay writer. But when a teacher puts words in front of me, I have to count them before I can read them. I like counting, and I'm a fast counter, but I don't have superhero abilities. I saw a scene in this old movie where a waitress drops a box of toothpicks, and this savant guy looks at the pile and tells her how many toothpicks are on the floor in a split second. I can't do that. It takes me time to total the number of words on the page and the number of letters in the words. I'm sure I'm faster than anyone else in 3rd-period language arts, but my counting is extra work that doesn't get me any extra credit.

So when Ms. Fleming hands out a short story, I try to count the words quickly. Unfortunately, she calls on me to read 1st.

"Lucy, please begin."

"I pass."

"Excuse me? What exactly are you passing on?" she asks, and the rest of the class laughs.

"Can't someone else read it?" I've only counted the words in the 1st paragraph. 192.

"I'm sure someone else *could* read it. But I asked you." She takes off her glasses. I'm not sure why. Maybe so I can see her evil stare more clearly.

I look down at the story. I count the words in the 2nd paragraph. Only 27. For a total of 219.

"You may begin, Lucy." Ms. Fleming interrupts my counting of the 3rd paragraph. More of the class laughs. I blink a lot to keep my eyes from getting too wet.

I read the 1st paragraph slowly. I pause after each sentence and try to count more words. I can't. I reach the bottom of paragraph 2 and stop.

"Very nice," Ms. Fleming says. "Continue, please."

The next paragraph is long. I push myself hard to count all the words so I can read. Kids around me murmur. Ms. Fleming sighs heavily. My head feels light and my cheeks hot. I lose my spot in the jumble of words. I have to start over.

"I lost my place," I whisper. I'm not talking about the words but the count. I need the count. My eyes move quickly over the 1st few lines, reconfirming their totals.

1st line, 17.

2nd line, 22.

3rd line, also 22.

4th . . .

"I'll read," someone calls out.

"Fine," Ms. Fleming says. "Take over, Windy. And, Lucy, I'd like to speak to you after class."

I let out a breath and sink into my seat. I don't worry about what excuse I'll give Ms. Fleming at the end of class. I just count.

We finish reading the story as a class. Then we form groups to discuss the theme. I'm grouped with 3 girls I haven't met yet. They make me the secretary, which means I have to write everything down—and do all the actual work—while they talk about some boys I don't know. I try my best to answer the questions written on the Smart Board.

After class, I stick around as Ms. Fleming ordered. She seems to forget about me until I start walking toward the door.

"Lucy," she calls out. "Do you want to explain your reluctance to participate in class?"

I shrug.

"You're a very smart girl."

"What do you mean?" I shouldn't respond. I should be quiet and nod.

Ms. Fleming's eyebrows shoot up. "I mean, you seem like a smart girl."

She knows nothing about me. It's just teacher talk. That's a relief. Life is easier when there are no expectations.

"You're plenty capable of succeeding in this class. But you will need to participate, follow the rules, and do the work."

I was the only 1 in my discussion group who did any work. Ms. Fleming doesn't seem to know this, or she doesn't care.

"Do you understand what's expected of you?" she asks.

"I just ... I don't like to read out loud. The words get jumbled in my head or my mouth or something." I try to explain my problem without *really* explaining my problem, hoping she'll understand and maybe show some sympathy.

"Okay. This is something we can work on. A goal." She pulls off her glasses and puts them to her lips. "Wait 1 second."

She walks over to her desk and opens a blue folder. I'm already late for science. Everyone will watch me walk in and watch me sit.

"Here." She hands me 4 sheets that are stapled to-gether. "We'll be reading this story next week. You can practice reading it aloud so you're more comfortable."

"Thanks." I can count the words ahead of time, too. For a split second, I think about telling her the whole truth. I decide against it.

"And our 1st class novel will be *The Call of the Wild,* if you want to read ahead." She points to the piles of books on the back shelf.

"Thanks," I say again.

"You'll see, Lucy. By the end of the year, we will have you comfortable reading out loud." She gives me an en-couraging smile. I wish I could believe her, but I know I'll never be comfortable in this school.

14

I survive my 1st 2 weeks of middle school. Only 171 school days to go until summer break. We have homework for the weekend, but it's for language arts class, not math, so that's disappointing. Mr. Stoker thinks he's rewarding us by not giving homework on Fridays.

Windy and I share a bag of peanut M&M's on the bus ride home. I don't mind sharing, because she always uses hand sanitizer when I offer it.

"Hey, my mom said you can come over for a sleepover tomorrow night," Windy says. "Can you come?"

I don't know what to say. I've never spent the night at someone's house.

"Don't worry. I told her she has to clean really good for you and get Clorox wipes. A lot of them."

"You shouldn't have said that. She's going to think I'm a brat." And Windy knows I carry my own wipes everywhere. It's like she wants her mom to know I'm weird.

"No, she won't. So, can you come?"

"I'll have to ask my grandmother." I can't tell if the feeling in my gut is excitement. Someone's inviting me over. Or is it fear? So much could go wrong. Or maybe I haven't cleaned the desks enough at school and have finally caught some disease. I'm pretty sure I'm going to throw up.

"Why do you want me to sleep over?" I ask.

"It'll be fun."

"Okay."

Windy gets off the bus before I do. She says she'll call me in an hour to make plans. She needs to know if I'm allowed to watch R-rated movies or just PG-13, and if I can smuggle in candy.

Nana is thrilled to hear about the sleepover. Judging by her jumping around, you'd think I'd been invited to the White House. The next day, we argue about things we've never argued about before. Clothes.

"Not those pajamas." She makes a disgusted face. "They're ratty. Take the purple pj's with the owls."

"They're not comfortable," I say.

"They're cute."

Cute wins. But only because I don't feel like arguing any more.

"We're leaving in 5 minutes," she says. That gives me enough time to get online and explain my absence. I haven't missed a Saturday night math chat since February, and that was because we had an ice storm and didn't have power for 106 hours.

LightningGirl: it is with a heavy heart that I share this news

LightningGirl: I will be unavailable for the Saturday night math chat

LightningGirl: when I return in 18 hours I will comment on the topics discussed

I'm trying to sound professional, but judging by the reactions, I may have taken it too far.

SquareHead314: LG, is everything OK?

Numberlicious: sounds serious

HipHypotenuse: you're in my thoughts and prayers

LightningGirl: I'm OK

LightningGirl: ttyl—or tomorrow

∞

Windy lives in a neighborhood where every home has a sign in the bushes advertising its brand of security system. Her house is 3 stories tall, with real pillars out front.

"Nice place," Nana says as we walk past the rosebushes and onto the porch. I go to ring the doorbell with my elbow, but Windy opens the door before I get a chance.

"I've been waiting all day." Windy yanks me in by the arm. "Come in," she says to Nana.

"Hey." I tap my toe 3 times.

"Look! Hand sanitizer. Right near the door. Just like at your place." It's the only thing about Windy's house that is *just like my place*. She gives me 2 squirts.

"Thanks."

Windy picks up a paper from the same table and puts it in my face.

"Here's a list of everything we are going to do."

She holds it too close for me to read. I can see that she's numbered the activities, all 31 of them.

"Okay," I say. I probably don't sound okay. I can't catch my breath.

"Mrs. Callahan, is Lucy allowed to dye her hair?" Windy asks.

"Um ...," Nana says. "Are your parents home?"

"My mom is," Windy answers. Then she turns around and yells into the quiet house, "Mom! Lucy's grandma wants to talk to you."

Windy turns back to us with a smile. "My father doesn't live here anymore. My mom kicked him out last year. I'm not supposed to know the reason, but I do. Do you want me to tell you?"

"No," Nana answers.

Ms. Sitton walks into the foyer before Windy can share any family secrets. Her shoes click on the hardwood floor. 1-2, 3-4, 5-6, 7-8. She's tall and thin and very put together—like with makeup and jewelry and high heels. Her black skirt and pink shirt (the color of 11) make me think she's dressed for something important or that *she* is really important. She looks nothing like Windy.

"Hello." She holds out her hand to Nana. "I'm Adele Sitton."

"Barb Callahan."

"Thank you so much for allowing Lucy to come over," Ms. Sitton says. "I've heard so much about her."

That makes my stomach hurt. What does she know? What did Windy say? Did she Google search me?

"Lucy is very excited," Nana says.

"Great." Ms. Sitton puts her hands over Windy's ears. "Windy has a hard time making friends."

"I can still hear you, Mom." Windy pushes her away.

The adults exchange phone numbers, and Ms. Sitton asks if I have any allergies. I don't. Then it's time for good-bye.

"Have fun," Nana says. "Call me if you need anything." She kisses my cheek. Suddenly, I think I might cry, which is stupid because I'm only going to be gone 18 hours. I look at my watch. 17 hours and 41 minutes. I miss my bed. I miss my room. My computer. My nana. My ratty pajamas.

I close my eyes and recite the numbers of pi in my head.

"You okay?" Windy asks, grabbing my shoulder.

"Yeah." I tap my toe 3 times to stop the flow of numbers.

"Come on." She gives me a tour of the house, which doesn't include many details. "Dining room, living room, fancy living room with no TV, Mom's room, kitchen." All of them are huge.

I count the stairs as we walk up—18—and don't touch the handrail. Windy has an older sister named Cherish, who isn't home. The upstairs belongs to them. They each have a bedroom. There's a study with 2 desks, and the walls are lined with bookshelves (I want to count all the books, but we don't stop), and a room she calls FROG, with a big TV, beanbag chairs, a video game system, and a shelf of board games.

"FROG?" I ask. There isn't an aquarium, and it isn't decorated with Kermit pictures or lily pads.

"Family room over garage. FROG."

I guess it's a term you only learn if you own a mansion.

"So, what should we do 1st?" Windy asks. She takes my bag and puts it down in the corner. A container of Clorox wipes sits on her dresser. Across the top is written *For Lucy.*

"I thought you had a list." I tap my toe 3 times.

"I do." She smiles. "I was trying to be polite."

"Whatever you want to do." I don't mean whatever. There are plenty of things that I would never do. Like share a fork or eat in a restaurant with a sanitation rating lower than A.

The purple walls of Windy's room are covered with an odd combination of adorable save-the-animal pictures and Broadway musical posters. A bulletin board filled with ticket stubs and photos hangs above her bed.

"Is that Maddie?" I ask, pointing to a picture taken on a beach. I already know the answer. It's definitely Maddie. She's in 6 pictures—camping, birthday party, roller-skating, Girl Scouts, soccer team, dance class.

Windy moves closer and squints. "Oh yeah. Our moms are good friends, so we hang out sometimes."

"Really?"

"Well, we used to."

"What happened?" I ask.

Windy shrugs. "We're still kind of friends. She's just super popular now."

And the worst person I've ever met.

"So, what are we going to do?" I ask, changing the subject.

"Manis and pedis." She holds up 2 bottles of nail polish. "It's the best brand. Never tested on animals."

"Okay? But can we wash our hands 1st?"

"Sure."

A few minutes later, we're painting each other's nails

to the soundtrack of *Newsies*. We both have very sad nails, short and broken. Windy paints mine lime green (like the number 41), and I paint hers bright pink (a shade lighter than the number 21).

"You're not very good at this." Windy laughs. "You keep getting polish on my knuckles."

"Sorry," I say. "I've never painted anyone's nails before." It's also hard because I try not to hold her hand while running the brush over each nail 3 times.

"Really? I guess I've been in training since the moment I was born. My mom owns 2 day spas. She's all about looking good and feeling good. She's in her 40s, and she still wears a bikini when we go to the beach."

"She's very pretty," I say.

"I know, and I don't look anything like her." Windy slowly shakes her head. "Lucky for her, she has my sister. You can see the shared DNA in their long eyelashes and small butts."

"You have nice eyelashes," I say, hoping to make her feel better. I've never really noticed her eyelashes behind her glasses. They're nice enough.

"Whatever. I'm pretty sure I was switched at birth. At least I hope so. I look forward to meeting my real mom someday. I'll know her when I see her. In 1 hand she'll be carrying a bag of peanut butter cups, and in the other, a Greenpeace sign."

"I think your mom's nice."

"Whatever." Windy rolls her eyes. "What about your parents? Where are they? Dead or something?"

"Yeah."

"Oh my god, I'm sorry. I didn't mean—"

I hold up a hand to stop her apology. "It's okay. My mom died of ovarian cancer when I was a baby. I don't remember her. And I never knew my dad. He didn't stick around." Uncle Paul says my dad split 2 seconds after the pregnancy test came back positive, and that it was a good decision for all of us—especially me.

Windy's eyebrows lift high on her face, and her lips turn down. "Lucy, I'm so sorry. You're like an orphan."

I laugh. "Stop. Please. I'm not an orphan." I've thought of myself as a genius, a savant, and a freak, but never an orphan. Nana has always been there, and Uncle Paul, too. "I'm fine. I don't need you to collect canned goods for me or give me a coat for winter. I have a family. Don't turn me into a Cougars Care Project."

Windy opens another bottle of nail polish. It's bright yellow (like the number 2). "I guess we could help other less fortunate orphans. Unless you've had any ideas about our project?"

"Not really. We still need another person in our group." The school said we should be a team of 3 or 4. Obviously, I would vote for 3.

"I'm still working on it. It's hard to find the perfect candidate."

When Windy finishes, my hands look great. On top of each lime-green nail, she's painted a yellow lightning bolt.

"Like your necklace," she says. "You always wear it."

"I *am* Lightning Girl." The name slips out of my mouth before my brain thinks about what I'm saying.

She tilts her head. "What does that mean?"

"It's a nickname my uncle Paul gave me," I lie. He only calls me *genius*.

"Why?"

"When I was little, I ran around a lot. And I was fast." The lies keep coming.

Windy shrugs and checks out her own manicure. It looks like I put on her polish with an old toothbrush. But she doesn't complain. "I know what we can do next." She pulls out a book from a drawer in her desk. *101 Things You Never Knew About Your Best Friend*. I know you're not supposed to judge a book by its cover—and probably not by its title, either—but I instantly want to give it 2 thumbs up or 5 stars. (I'm not sure what scale is used to measure excellence in literature.) There's a prime number in the title, and the words *best friend*. No one has ever called me a best friend. Windy hands me a purple pen (like the number 3)—which I wipe down—and she grabs an aqua pen (that's similar to 75). And we get to work.

I learn Windy wants to be an environmental lawyer, she's afraid of hot-air balloons, and her favorite quote is not from a musical but from a movie. Dumbledore in *Harry Potter and the Chamber of Secrets:* "It is not our abilities that show what we truly are. It is our choices." I worry she might know *my* ability and my secret, and quoting Einstein will only make her more suspicious. So I lie and say my favorite quote is Dory's famous line from *Finding Nemo:* "Just keep swimming." She nods like this makes complete sense.

We finish the book. We eat gluten-free fake-cheese pizza. We watch 3 movies, including a horror flick, while munching on unbuttered popcorn and the gummy bears I brought from home. We sleep with the lights on. We make plans to do it all again next weekend.

And I only think about my online math chat 3 times. That is about 80 percent less than I normally would in an 18-hour period.

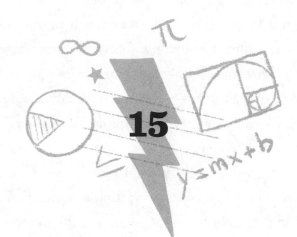

By Thursday, Windy has asked 7 girls to join our team. Each turned her down. Most said they were already on a team, and 1 said she wasn't doing it. Her dad was a doctor, and he wrote an excuse. Such a big project would cause her anxiety.

On the bus, Windy asks, "Did you come up with any ideas for our project?" Last night, she assigned me a task—come up with at least 20 possibilities.

"Nothing good." I had only 3, and I knew she wouldn't like any of them.

Unclean cafeteria tables
Unclean desks
Unclean doorknobs

"That's okay. I've got some great ideas. What do you think of starting an all-girls school in Zambia?" she asks, completely serious.

I shrug. "I wouldn't know how."

"I'm sure we could figure it out." She opens her notebook. "But I have other ideas, too." She reads me her list. Every suggestion is a huge project that would require a few million dollars and a team of experts. She wants to build a library in downtown Baltimore or open a women's hospital in India or run a search-and-rescue team that would rush to victims of tsunamis.

"Well, what do you think?" she asks.

"I think we need something closer to home. My grandmother probably won't let me leave the country. Maybe we could collect aluminum cans and recycle them."

Windy makes a gagging sound. "Picking up trash? Really? That's not original at all."

"I wasn't offering to pick up trash." Now I make a gagging sound.

"The only thing more unoriginal is helping puppies find homes." She falls back in the seat and takes out a pen.

"I wouldn't want to do that, either. I don't even like puppies. Except on calendars and coffee mugs." Animals are unpredictable, and they can't be wiped down with Clorox.

She laughs. "Don't worry. I'll come up with something perfect."

"And realistic?"

She shrugs. Windy likes to think big, and she needs someone else to pull her back to earth. I'm her gravity.

In math, Mr. Stoker starts class not with a review of the homework, like he always does, but with a lecture on math in the real world. And it's awesome.

While he's talking, I imagine showing him my world. He'd love to see math and numbers the way I do—in everything from the stars to building construction to ripples on a lake. Even water draining in the sink. I see circles and bisecting triangles that form equations in my brain. If only there were an easy way, like wearing special glasses; a lightning strike is too painful, and results aren't guaranteed.

"Engineering, science, finance, computer development, teaching, banking. These all require mathematics." He leans forward on his stool. "But so do government, art, writing, love."

"Love?" Maddie asks.

"Yes. There's a mathematician named Hannah Fry. She's created an equation for finding your soul mate." Mr. Stoker does air quotes around *soul mate*. "She used the optimal stopping theory."

I know optimal stopping theory. It's a way to calculate the best time to do something, to figure out the best odds. It's usually used in finance or pricing, not romance.

"Say, as an average adult, you date 20 people. And 1 of those 20 is your best fit for a spouse. Each time you date a person, you essentially must decide do I marry this guy, do I marry this gal, or do I move on. The next person could be better, or he or she could be worse. Optimal stopping theory proposes this solution.... Get it? *Proposes?*"

We give Mr. Stoker a few pity laughs.

He continues explaining by drawing little stick men and women on the whiteboard. I don't mean to judge my classmates, but if I had to guess, I think Mr. Stoker's lesson goes over their heads.

"No thanks," Maddie says, and maybe she does get it. She's actually pretty smart. Evil but smart. "I'd rather try online dating than leave it up to this math theory."

"This is not a guarantee. But it is a way to maximize your success. With optimal stopping theory, you're 3 times more likely to pick your soul mate than if you were to randomly select 1 person from your field of 20 candidates."

"How romantic," Jennifer says.

"This country's divorce rate is over 50 percent. Maybe OST could help." Mr. Stoker continues talking about math as the basis of life. From cells to music. Numbers and patterns control our world and can make it better.

"Mathematics is even being used in the courtroom.

With enough data from similar cases, a verdict can be determined with amazing accuracy. Maybe lawyers will eventually be obsolete."

"My mom is a lawyer," Maddie calls out. "I wouldn't say that around her."

Mr. Stoker ignores the interruption. "Now, these concepts are big and complicated. But I encourage you to remember the power of mathematics as you work on your service projects. Don't be afraid of numbers. Use them to compute your solutions. Look at the world as it is intended."

He gives us the last 10 minutes of the period to work on our projects. Windy drags her chair over to my desk.

"We need to use math," I say as she sits down.

"You want to save puppies and use math?" Windy asks.

"I never said anything about puppies." I shake my head. "But, yes, we definitely need to use math. And Mr. Stoker needs to be our faculty mentor."

"I have a math problem for you," she says. "We are still a group of 2. And I think everyone already has a group."

We look around the room. It's hard to tell whether everyone is already on a team; they could be working with someone in another class.

"I've already asked Peyton, Margery, Kaitlyn, Sarah, and Maddie," Windy says.

And since Windy's not good at whispering, Maddie

looks up from her cell phone, which she's playing with under her desk. She glares at us for even saying her name.

"You asked Maddie? Did you really think she'd want to be on my team?" I'm sure Maddie would rather eat slugs than work with me. And I feel the same way, but I would never eat a slug. I don't even like shrimp.

Windy shrugs. "I think she would have joined us if she hadn't already said yes to Daniela and Jasmine. They've started their project."

I stare at Windy to see if she's joking. She doesn't seem to be. I shake my head.

"Actually, I've asked everyone." She taps her fingers on my Clorox-cleaned desk.

It would have been easier if the teachers assigned the teams, like Mrs. Shields did in social studies class for our Egypt project. But then I probably wouldn't have been with Windy.

Windy puts her hand in the air and waves Mr. Stoker over like he's a waiter.

"Yes, ladies?" Mr. Stoker says when he gets to my desk.

"Will you be our mentor?" I speak before Windy does.

He grins. "I thought you'd never ask. What are you considering as a—"

"Mr. Stoker," Windy says, "we can't find another team member. I have asked literally every person in the 7th grade. So I think it is only fair if Lucy and I are a team of 2. Is that okay?"

"You've asked *literally* everyone?" he says.

"Yes."

Mr. Stoker clears his throat. "Excuse me, ladies and gentlemen. Does everyone have a service project team?"

"See," Windy says right away. "Everyone is—"

"I need a team," Levi interrupts. He doesn't look up from the notebook he's doodling in.

"Great. You can join Lucy and Windy." Mr. Stoker taps the project sheet that sits on my desk. "Add Levi's name."

I hesitate. Levi's a cheater, and I still haven't gotten my revenge—other than not talking to him for 15 days. But Mr. Stoker stands over me, waiting. I cave and write Levi's name in pencil. It can always be erased.

"Good luck, team," Mr. Stoker says, and then walks over to Ethan.

"You have to actually do some work if you want to be on our team," Windy orders Levi.

He shrugs but says nothing.

"Do you have any ideas?" she asks.

"Nope." He never looks up from his notebook. I guess it doesn't matter. There are only 2 minutes left in class, and Windy will probably make all the decisions anyway.

16

Windy has ordered that our group meet at lunch on Monday. She and I get permission to go straight to the media center from science. Levi tells us he'll catch up. I wipe a small section of the table and then make the mistake of looking at the cloth. It's grimier than when I clean my usual spot at lunch. I use extra hand sanitizer and make Windy take some, too. We share my sandwich, cookies, and chips, even though you're not supposed to eat in here. We keep the food hidden behind a stack of books.

"Would you still be my friend if I didn't always have candy and cookies?" I ask her.

"Of course," she says. "But maybe not best friends."

I know she's joking. Is that a sign of being real friends? When you know something they say should be followed by "JK."

After we finish our high-sugar foods, Windy starts to panic. I should carry extra Jolly Ranchers to keep her calm in situations like this.

"He's not coming. I knew it. I'm going to talk to Mr. Stoker and get Levi kicked off our team. It's not fair that we have to do all the work."

We haven't really done any work yet.

"Lunch period isn't over," I say. "He could still come." With only 8 minutes left, I'm starting to have my doubts, too.

"I don't know why we let him on our team."

"We didn't have a choice," I remind her. "And I didn't want him, either. He's a cheater."

"You make it sound like he's your boyfriend and he kissed someone else."

"Gross."

Windy slumps back in her chair. "Maddie's group has a great project. We need a great project."

"What's theirs?" I ask, but I don't really want to know.

"Filling backpacks with school supplies for refugee families. They have a goal of 200 backpacks for kids in kindergarten all the way through high school. And they're not just going to have notebooks and pencils and stuff like that. But also gift cards so kids can buy new shoes."

"That's cool."

"Yeah, it is." She stares off into space.

I get the feeling Windy wants to be on Team Maddie. Maybe I should suggest it. Free her from our agreement to be partners. If Maddie is only working with Jasmine and Daniela, they have room for 1 more.

"Windy, if you want to—"

"Look who's finally here." Windy sits up and points toward the door.

Levi slides 2 books into the return slot. Then he talks to the librarian for a minute before walking over to us and collapsing into the chair next to mine.

"So, what are we doing for this project?" he asks.

"Where have you been?" Windy asks.

"A growing boy has got to eat." He pats his stomach.

Windy glares at him. "I can't believe you are so—"

"Let's work on the project," I interrupt. "Okay?"

"Fine. Here are my suggestions." Windy opens her notebook. She has 2 new pages of ideas, and she reads each outrageous proposal.

Levi groans. "Do you have anything reasonable in there?"

"With some work, they're all reasonable."

Levi scans the list. "Protecting sea lions from motorboats. How is that reasonable?"

"We could put up signs and warn boaters that they are killing sea lions."

"We live 3 hours from the ocean. I've never even seen a sea lion."

Windy shuts her notebook and slaps it on the table. "Lucy is the 1 who wants to save animals."

"What? No, I don't. No animals, please." I wave my hands like I'm stopping traffic. "I suggested picking up cans on the side of the road." Assuming I can find industrial-grade rubber gloves.

"Save the animals. That isn't a problem," Levi says. "It's a bumper sticker."

"I don't want to save animals," I say again, but neither Windy nor Levi is listening to me.

"Okay. How about this? Find animals loving, caring forever homes. Is *that* a bumper sticker?" she asks Levi.

"A really crappy 1."

Windy rolls her eyes.

"We still need to be more specific," I say. "Like what kind of animals do you want to save, Windy?"

"Dogs and cats," she says. But I know she'd rather save black rhinos or narwhals.

"Are you discriminating against snakes and turtles? Do they not need loving, caring forever homes?" Levi asks.

Windy puts a finger in Levi's face. "I think the problem is that you make fun of everything I say."

"Shhh!" Mrs. Wilson snaps at us from behind the checkout desk. "The media center is a privilege."

"Sorry," Windy says.

"Just write whatever you want," Levi says with a fake smile, and I notice the gap between his front teeth. "This doesn't count for anything. We're still going to pass 7th grade even if we have a loser project."

"You're giving up already?" Windy asks.

"Not giving up. Giving in. There's a difference." Levi throws his backpack onto the table.

Windy groans.

I'm starting to think working on a team is a form of torture. The teachers are doing this as part of a weird social experiment to see if they can make students hate each other.

Levi opens his backpack and pulls out his camera. He plays with the buttons, then aims it at Windy. Her scowl turns into a sweet smile, as if he has figured out how to tame her. When he points the camera in my direction, I hide behind a science textbook.

"Is this for your site?" Windy asks, hopeful.

Levi reviews Windy's picture on the back of the camera. "Probably not." He presses the red delete button.

I have no idea what they're talking about, but Windy looks ready to strangle Levi again.

"You're not allowed to take pictures during school," she hisses. "It's in the handbook. I could report you."

"Whatever. It's for art class. And you're not supposed to eat in here." He holds up my empty potato chip bag.

"Back to work," I jump in. "We need to state our project as a problem. A problem with numbers."

"I hate math," Levi mumbles.

I jerk back like I've been slapped. "That's the stupidest thing you've ever said."

He gives me a questioning look. "Sorry?"

"Math makes sense. So maybe we could use numbers to express our problem and even the solution."

"How?" Windy asks.

"Like there are 1,000 animals put down in our county every month." I make up that number, which is not something I usually do. It makes my stomach hurt.

"Oh my god! There are?" Windy snaps forward in a panic.

"I don't know. I was trying to give an example. It's probably much, much less." I'll have to look up the number when I get home. I hate imprecise descriptions like *lots, few,* and *hardly any.*

"This is turning into a really morbid project," Levi says. "Counting dead animals."

"How about this? Only *x* number of animals are adopted each month from the local shelter."

"Is that a problem?" Levi asks. "Sounds like a statement." At least he doesn't call me a bumper sticker.

"It's a problem if another 200 are waiting to be adopted." Again, I'm making up numbers that I know nothing about. It feels like cheating.

"I got it," Windy says. She writes and talks at the same time. "On average, the Hamlin County Animal Control has 1,000 dogs and cats waiting to be adopted, and the shelter can only hold 500." Now she's making up numbers. I'm spreading a disease of inaccuracy.

"I guess that works. I'll look up the actual number tonight. It could be a good project."

"Levi?" Windy wants his input.

"Whatever." That counts as a yes from Levi.

"And the solution is easy," Windy adds. "We help the animals get adopted." She smiles. I know she's excited, and we don't even need to go to Africa.

"Or we help the county build a bigger animal prison," Levi says, and Windy glares at him.

"Shut up. We're going to save thousands of animals. Like it or not. Right, Lucy?"

"I guess." I'm not sure what just happened. I never wanted to work with animals. I still don't. I only wanted Windy and Levi not to kill each other. I guess I solved 1 problem.

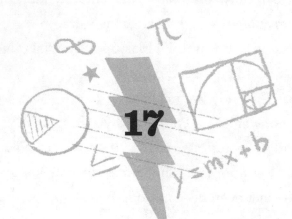

Finding the exact information I want about the animal shelter is impossible. On the Hamlin County Animal Control website, it says the department finds homes for 95 percent of the healthy dogs and 78 percent of the healthy cats. It doesn't say what happens to the other 5 percent of dogs or 22 percent of cats. And it doesn't explain what *healthy* means.

So I call their office.

"Hamlin County Animal Control," a woman answers. "How may I help you?"

"Hi, my name is Lucy Callahan, and I have some questions for a school project."

"What kind of questions?"

"How many dogs can your shelter hold? How many dogs get adopted each month? How many cats can you hold? How many cats—"

"All that information is available on the website."

"No, it's not. I have the website open in front of me."

"Then it's not public information. I'm sorry." She doesn't sound sorry.

"You don't know how many dogs you have there?" I ask. "You just have to count."

"That's not my job. My job is to answer the phone. You're welcome to visit and count the animals." She's ready to hang up.

"Wait. What does the website mean by *healthy*?"

"Excuse me?"

"Your website says that 95 percent of healthy dogs get adopted. What does that mean?"

"Um … out of the healthy animals that we recover or are surrendered, we find homes for 95 percent of them."

"What happens to the sick animals?" I ask. "Like the animals with brain damage."

The woman is quiet. I want her to say that they go to special homes where they are cared for.

"I don't have an answer for that. I do know that our adoption hours are Tuesday through Saturday from 10 to 7, and Sundays noon to 5."

"We just want to help."

She lets out a noisy breath. "Volunteer information is

also on the website. But you must be at least 16 years old or accompanied by a parent. Are you 16?"

"No."

"Thank you for your call. Please spay or neuter your pets." The line goes quiet.

That was a waste of 4 minutes.

Frustrated, I call Windy and tell her we can't save the animals. We aren't old enough. I'm kind of relieved.

"I'll fix this," Windy says with complete confidence.

"How?" I ask.

"You'll see. There are other animal shelters that would love to have us."

"If you say so." I'm hoping she's wrong.

"Hey, have you checked out Levi's page lately?"

"What page?"

"ArtBoom. It's a website where people post paintings and pictures. It's supposed to be like an online art gallery. I think it's kind of dumb."

"Never heard of it."

"You should look at it. There are a lot of you."

"Really?" My stomach drops.

"His user name is Levi123."

I say good-bye to Windy and find Levi's page on Art-Boom. Windy may have exaggerated. There are only 3 pictures of me out of 45 (6.667 percent). Maybe it seems like a lot because there is only 1 of Windy (2.222 percent).

His gallery is divided into 5 folders—*bored, curious, angry, hurt, peaceful*—and each has multiple black-and-white photos. I'm under *curious* twice and *angry* once. That's the picture from Mr. Stoker's room after I was accused of cheating. Windy's picture is in the *bored* tab. Her chin is resting in her hand and she's staring out the window instead of at the book in front of her.

There's a gold star in the corner of Levi's page. It's been selected as *Best of the Month* by the ArtBoom community.

I click each picture to view it at full size. Even without the labels typed across the top of the page, I could've guessed the emotion for every picture. Levi sees things in an instant that I must miss every day.

When I enlarge 1 of the pictures under the *hurt* tab, I'm surprised to see it's Maddie. I almost didn't recognize her. Her dark hair covers half her face, and her arms are wrapped around her chest like she's cold. The other people in the background are out of focus, but I can tell she's in the cafeteria. *What was happening that day?* There are no tears … yet. Levi's captured that split second before her eyes fill. I can imagine that a moment later she was running off to the bathroom to be alone.

Levi and I live in the same world, but we see things very differently. I guess it would be boring if we all had the same view.

Later that night, when Nana and I are watching TV, my phone vibrates. I shouldn't have doubted Windy. She's pushing our project forward.

Windy: The Pet Hut

Windy: tomorrow after school

Windy: my sister will drive us

Levi: whatever

18

Windy's sister, Cherish, picks us up after school—as promised. Windy sits in the front of the car. Levi and I get in the back. Cherish watches through her rearview mirror as I sit, stand, sit, stand, sit. She raises her perfect eyebrows.

"You've got 1 hour," Cherish says to Windy as we pull out of the school parking lot.

"2," Windy insists.

"No, 1," Cherish says. "Mom said I had to drop you off and pick you up in an hour."

"We will call you when we're done," Windy says. She seems to argue with everyone but me.

It only takes 11 minutes to drive to the Pet Hut. We pass 4 traffic lights, 147 telephone poles (out the right-hand window), and 17 fire hydrants. When we get out of the car, Cherish shouts to us, "1 hour!"

We stand in the empty parking lot and stare at the single-story red building with windows across the front.

"This used to be a Pizza Hut," Levi says, pulling a camera from his bag. "That's disgusting."

"It's not like it was an animal shelter and pizza place at the same time," Windy says. "Come on."

We follow her to the side door, where the old logo still shows on the glass.

I let Windy hold the door open for me. My plan is to touch nothing. But in case that doesn't work, I have a new pack of Clorox wipes and some extra hand sanitizer in my bag.

I tap my toe 3 times.

The place smells of wet newspaper, and the entrance is crowded with bags of dog and cat food, old blankets folded and stacked, and empty animal crates of different sizes. Muffled barking echoes through the walls.

"Can I help you?" a guy behind the counter asks. A menu over his head still has pictures of sodas and pizza, but the written information (all 11 words, 10 digits, and 3 dollar signs) is about pet pricing.

ADOPTION FEES
PUPPIES $200
DOGS $175
CATS $90
APPLICATION REQUIRED. MUST BE AT LEAST 18.

"Do you work here?" Windy sounds like she's testing him.

"I volunteer here." His long dark hair looks knotted, and he has huge holes in his earlobes. His skin is white, and his nose is crooked and has a diamond stud. He's older than we are—in high school at least.

"Is Claire Barrington here?" Windy asks.

"Yeah. Hang on." He hops off his stool and opens the heavy metal door at the end of the counter.

The barking grows louder. I step back. I've never been around dogs or any animals. Dogs aren't clean and don't respect personal space—from what I've seen on TV. Some people claim that dogs' mouths are cleaner than humans' mouths. That's not true. Both are hot, wet, dark pools of bacteria. Dogs have as much bacteria, just different kinds.

I suddenly feel like gargling.

"Claire, you have visitors," the guy yells over the barking.

"Send them in."

"I'll wait here," I say.

"No, you won't." Levi grabs my elbow. "You're not leaving me alone with Windy." We follow her through the doorway.

A woman waves to us from the far end of the room. She's leaning over a sink filled with bubbles and what seems to be a giant rat. She's wearing scrubs like a nurse. The pants are a pretty sky blue (similar to the number 4), and the top is purple (like the number 3) with kittens. Her red hair is pulled into a sloppy ponytail. Her skin's pale, but her cheeks are pink—I assume from fighting the giant rat in the sink.

We walk past 8 large kennels on the right. Each has a wild-looking dog inside. On top of the big kennels are 10 smaller cages with smaller dogs. The size of the dog doesn't matter. They all seem to be trying to break free. Like they want to chew my throat. I touch my lightning-bolt charm and keep my eyes forward.

"Hi, gang," she says. "I'm Claire. Owner, operator, CEO, and head shampooer of the Pet Hut. How can I help you?"

I tap my toe 3 times and try to hold my breath. Wet dog—or rat—has to be 1 of the worst smells in the world.

"We're doing a service project for school," Windy starts.

"Let me guess," Claire says. "East Hamlin Middle."

"How did you know?"

"I had a group of kids in here earlier this week."

"So not only is our idea boring, it's been done before," Levi says.

I roll my eyes. Like he doesn't mind copying off of other people.

"We will take all the help we can get," Claire says. "Why don't you tell me your names and what you have in mind?" She turns on the water and starts rinsing the small dog in the sink. Droplets land on my arm. My brain lets me see these perfect circles filled with triangles defined by the ratio pi. More beautiful math that surrounds me everywhere. Still, I'll need to shower when I get home. Who knows what germs lurk in those circles?

Windy takes care of the introductions. "That's Levi. He doesn't like anything. She's Lucy, the quiet and thoughtful 1. I'm Windy. I'm the leader of the group. I mean, not officially, but unofficially."

"I'd vote for that dog as group leader before I'd vote for you." Levi motions with his head toward a ceramic beagle that's holding open a door.

"See! He never says anything positive."

Claire forces a laugh. "Do you want to go to the office and I can answer your questions? Or we could start with a little tour, and I'll tell you about our needs."

"I've got questions," I say. It's easier not to touch anything if we stand in 1 spot.

"Tour," Levi votes. And for once Windy agrees with him.

"You can ask me questions while we walk," Claire says.

We wait for Claire to towel off the dog.

"What kind of dog is that?" Windy asks.

"He's a mutt, but our vet thinks he's part Chihuahua."

"And part shih tzu," Levi adds.

Claire nods. "That's what I was thinking, too."

"Look at the face and the longer fur. That's shih tzu," Levi says. "I guess the skinny legs and tail make the vet think Chihuahua."

I stare at Levi.

"What?" he says. "I like dogs."

"Do you have any pets?" Claire asks him.

"2 dogs. Cocker spaniels that my moms rescued. Chase and Buttons."

Claire gives the wet dog a kiss on the nose and then puts him in an empty kennel. "Be good, Rex."

Gross.

"So, this is the dog room. Obviously." Claire holds out her arms. "The big boys and girls get those luxury apartments, and our smaller friends get the penthouses."

"How many dogs can you have in here at once?" I ask.

"Depends," she answers. "If everyone got their own space, 18. Sometimes we make them double-bunk. We also have a special room for puppies. Puppies don't stay with us long. They're usually adopted pretty quickly."

"How quick?" I ask.

"As quick as our volunteers can finish reviewing the paperwork." She smiles.

"We don't just want to volunteer," Windy says. "We want to improve your shelter."

"Oh, really?" Claire puts a finger to her bottom lip.

"Do you realize that everything that comes out of your mouth sounds like an insult?" Levi says to Windy.

"Does not."

"Yes, it does." He nods. "You're really talented."

"Let's continue the tour, gang," Claire suggests. "I'll show you the cat area."

The cat room is smaller than the dog room, but it has more occupants, and it smells worse. Even worse than wet Chihuahua–shih tzu. I count 22 cats and no kittens.

"We don't usually take in kittens," Claire says, reading my mind. "There's another shelter, Whiskers. They're better equipped to handle them."

"How many animals get adopted every week?" I ask.

"Depends. Can be anywhere from 1 to 20," she says.

"What's the average?" I ask.

Claire shrugs. "I'm not certain, sweetheart. 3 or 4?"

"Is that the mean, median, or mode?" Most people use mean for average, but I want to be sure.

"It's a guess." She laughs. "I can show you our records. And you can mean, media, and mole the data yourself."

"It's mean, median, and mode," I correct.

Levi elbows me in the side and whispers, "She was joking with you."

"Oh."

"I don't want to look at the records," Windy says.

"You can help me with the dogs," Claire offers. "I still need to walk kennels 5 through 8."

Claire asks Noah, the guy with the holes in his ears, to show me to her office. It's more of a closet with 3 huge filing cabinets, a desk, and an ancient computer.

"Is all the adoption information on the computer?" I ask him.

"Most of it. Well, some of it." He scratches his knotted hair. "I've been volunteering here for 6 months. People fill out an adoption form. If I have time, I put it in the computer. But all the paperwork is filed by date in here." He pulls open a drawer in the filing cabinet. The 1st folder is 4 months old.

"All of it?"

He points at a stack on the desk. "Except for that pile. They need to be filed."

The data is all here. Our problem and the solution for our project are buried in these papers. But none of it is usable yet.

The front door chimes.

"Have fun," Noah says, and he leaves me alone with plenty to calculate. Which actually *is* fun to me.

19

"**L**ucy!"

"What?" I look up. Levi stands in the door-way, his camera hanging around his neck. "Did you take my picture?"

"Maybe." He steps inside. "Cherish will be here in a minute. Time to go."

"You shouldn't take someone's picture without asking."

He shrugs.

"And you shouldn't cheat!"

"Seriously? You're still upset that I copied off you on the 1st day of school?"

"It was the 2nd day, and yes. Mr. Stoker will never know it wasn't me. He'll always think that I might be the cheater."

"He doesn't think you're the cheater." Levi's eyes focus on the floor. "I told him it was me."

I jerk back in the chair. "When?"

"I don't know. Sometime that week."

"Why? I mean, we kind of got away with it." This doesn't make sense. He didn't have to say anything.

Levi shrugs again. "Whatever. He was going to figure it out anyway. You get good grades. I'm the 1 failing his class."

"You are?" I try to sound surprised. I've seen all 7 of Levi's grades. According to those, he's got a 69 average. He's not failing, yet.

"Never mind." He steps closer. "What are you doing?"

I flip over the piece of paper I've been scribbling numbers on.

"Are you doing homework?" he asks.

"Sort of." I shove the paper in my pocket and then coat my hands in sanitizer. I've only made it through 57 adoption applications, but the patterns are already clear. I need to come back.

We leave the office, walking past the dog kennels. Even with all the barking, I can hear people arguing in the lobby.

Levi holds the door open for me.

"It's because of your germ issues, not because I'm a gentleman," he says.

"I know. Still, thanks."

In the lobby, a woman in dirty jeans and a faded green T-shirt (like the number 14) is standing at the counter yelling at Noah. In 1 hand she has an e-cigarette, and in the other a leash. The dog at the end of it trembles and tries to hide between her thick legs.

"You gotta take him!" the woman yells.

I tap my toe 3 times and look into the parking lot. I don't see Cherish's car.

"Lady, that's not how this works." Noah stares at her hard.

"You're a shelter, ain't ya?" She points her cigarette at his nose.

Noah cocks his head. "I *ain't* a shelter. I'm a volunteer and a freakin' premed student. You need to fill out your forms, and we'll add you to the waiting list."

"I don't have time for that."

"What's going on?" Claire walks into the lobby with Windy right behind her.

"This woman is trying to surrender an unverified dog," Noah explains. "She thinks she can drop the animal off without following procedure."

Claire smiles. "I'm sorry. We can't just take any dog, ma'am. We are not the county animal control. This is a private, nonprofit shelter."

"Well, where do you get your dogs from?"

"I've explained this." Noah shakes his head. "I'm going on break." He hops over the counter and heads out the front door.

"You fill out a surrender form," Claire says. "Then 1 of our volunteers will visit y'all. We need to ensure that the dog is healthy and friendly."

Healthy? There's that word again. What does that mean for a dog?

"He's right here." The woman tugs hard on the leash and pulls the dog forward. The mutt tucks his tail and keeps his head low. He's short and looks like a fluffy beagle.

"If our staff thinks the animal can be adopted, we will put him on the waiting list."

"Waiting list? How long does that take?"

"Depends," Claire says.

Of course she doesn't have exact numbers. How could she, with her current filing system?

"We only have 18 kennels," Claire continues. "And they're all filled. We probably have 10 dogs ahead of him."

The woman groans. "I'm moving. My husband's lost his job. I can't pay to get my car fixed."

"I'm sorry," Claire says. "We want to help." She holds out a hand for the dog to sniff. He moves slowly closer until Windy sneezes. Then he jumps back behind the woman.

"Poor boy." Levi sits on the filthy floor right in front of him. "You're a good-looking dog."

"What kind of dog is he?" Windy asks.

Levi lifts his camera to take pictures. The dog puts his nose all over the lens.

"Heck if I know," the woman says. "He's just cute. And that's what we call him."

"I bet you'll find a home really quick," Levi says to the dog.

"I bet he will," Claire agrees.

"Fine. Give me them papers," the woman growls.

"Certainly." Claire hands her a clipboard.

"Can you hold this?" The woman offers the leash to Levi.

"Sure."

She uncaps a pen with her teeth and starts writing. The phone rings, and as Claire walks behind the counter to answer it, suddenly—like it was all planned—the woman drops the clipboard and runs out the front door. She isn't very fast, but it's not like Windy or I can tackle her.

"Wait!" Claire yells.

The woman doesn't. The dog tries to run, too, but Levi holds on to the leash.

Noah comes back in. "Did that woman just ditch her dog?"

"Yes."

"Should we call the police?" Windy asks, pulling out

her cell phone. I don't think an actual crime has been committed.

"No," Claire says. "This happens a lot. I'll drive the dog over to animal control."

"Really?" Levi asks.

"But they might kill him," Windy says.

"Euthanize. And that's a last resort," Claire corrects. "Lucy, can you hand me the clipboard?"

I bend to pick it up. I avoid looking at the dog that might be sentenced to death. With only 2 fingers, I turn the clipboard over. The woman didn't get very far. She only wrote the animal's name.

Cutie Pi.

I stop and stare at the paper, like I might be reading it wrong.

Pi is spelled like the mathematical expression, not the pastry. I don't know if the woman is a bad speller or was just in a hurry. Still, I feel this is a sign. Nana sees signs in everything. Sometimes the cosmos or God is trying to tell us something. Like if she finds a dollar, which means God wants her to buy a lotto ticket. Other than being struck by lightning, I've never gotten a sign from God. But that was a pretty big 1.

"Pi?" I whisper the dog's name, and he turns to look at me. That's when I notice that 1 of the black spots on his back is the shape of a lightning bolt.

Another sign!

"You have to keep this dog." I can't help it—the words pop out.

"We really can't," Claire says. "There's no room."

"We can put him in a travel kennel until something opens up," Noah suggests. He kicks a large crate near the door.

"We're not supposed to—"

"Please," I say. "Do this and we'll enter all your adoption papers into the computer."

Claire's face softens. "You will?"

"We will?" Windy asks.

I nod. "Every last 1."

"I don't know...."

"Please." I'm about to get on my knees and really beg. But Claire saves me the trouble.

"Okay." She hands us each a volunteer permission slip. It's shorter than the dog adoption form. "Welcome to the Pet Hut team."

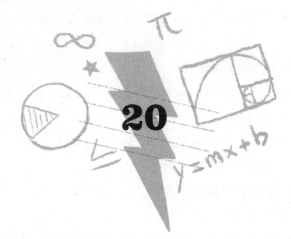

20

On Friday, we turn in the 2nd part of our project to Mr. Stoker before school.

"So, you're going to volunteer at the Pet Hut?" he asks.

"Lucy volunteered us to work in data entry," Windy whines. She told me last night and again this morning on the bus that she thought our project was boring.

"They don't have a good system," I say. "Most of their information is still on paper."

"So the problem is that the shelter has an antiquated filing system, and the solution is that you are going to update it?" Mr. Stoker asks.

"I guess," Windy says. "It was Lucy's idea."

"She had a good reason," Levi adds. It's true that I did it to save a dog. But I'm really excited to get all the numbers and data. By looking through only 57 applications, I've already seen trends. Small dogs are adopted almost 2 times as fast as big dogs, at least in my sample.

"You don't like this project, Windy?" Mr. Stoker asks.

She shrugs. "I want to do something bigger."

"Like?"

"We could run an adoption fair at Liberty Park," Windy says. "We could bring the dogs out to meet people."

"Okay." Mr. Stoker nods.

"Or the shelter always needs people to take the dogs for walks so that they get exercise." The place has a designated walking trail in the back. You have to pick up dog poop in a plastic bag. Something I'm probably not physically capable of doing.

Mr. Stoker doesn't say anything, so Windy keeps talking.

"Maybe we could set up a program for retired people or homeschooled kids to go in and exercise and play with the animals. Or we could organize a pet-food drive at school. Students could donate bags of food, and teachers could give them homework passes as a reward."

"All your ideas are great," Mr. Stoker says. "But you need buy-in from everyone in the group. Give it some more thought. How can you help the shelter? How can each of you get something out of the experience?"

"That's what I keep telling them." It doesn't take much to get Windy excited. "We can change lives. We can make a huge difference for the animals and their future owners and the whole town."

Levi groans.

"Do you have any thoughts?" Mr. Stoker asks Levi.

"I like hanging out with the dogs." He shrugs. "And I want to see them find homes."

"Can you bring me some more ideas by next Friday?" He looks at Levi and then at me.

"Definitely," Windy answers.

"Great." Mr. Stoker stands up. The homeroom bell rings on cue.

"We'll talk about this at lunch," Windy says. She takes our papers and goes to her desk.

"Can't wait." Levi glares at the back of Windy's head. Our team may not survive this project.

"Be nice," I whisper. I need them to not kill each other long enough that I can finish playing with numbers from the Pet Hut.

I move to my assigned seat. I sit, stand, sit, stand, sit and wipe down my desk. No one really notices anymore. It's only weird now if we have a substitute.

After the morning announcements, Mr. Stoker returns

our math tests from Tuesday. He lays them facedown on our desks.

"The average grade was 82. The highest grade was 95, and the lowest was 60." He gives us this data after every test. The class is averaging an 83.75 so far, not including homework. I wish my classmates would get it together and pull up their grades. I want to be average, but I also want an A. I have to think about colleges for next year, and they will want to see more than my SAT scores.

When Mr. Stoker gets to my desk, he leans over and says, "Nice job. A 92. Again."

I look up. He raises his eyebrows and shrugs like he can't explain the coincidence that is my math grade. Maybe next time I'll ace it. And then I'll blow 1. Then I'll ace 2 more. I just have to be careful not to set up a pattern.

Levi groans when he sees his grade. He got the 60. He flips his test over and starts to doodle on the back.

Mr. Stoker moves to the front of the room. "Let's go over the test."

He uses the overhead projector to put up the 1st 3 questions. Immediately, I see he's made a mistake in the 2nd question. I got number 2 wrong on my test. But I did it on purpose. Did Mr. Stoker?

He runs through the 1st problem. I play nervously with my lightning-bolt necklace.

"Any questions?"

The class is quiet except for an exaggerated yawn from the back row. Then Mr. Stoker walks through the 2nd problem, outlining the steps with his red marker.

Stop! That's wrong.

I don't say anything. I can't.

I stare at Maddie, willing her to speak up. She's the smartest kid in the class after me, but she doesn't seem to be paying attention.

"Any question on number 2? Most of you got this problem wrong."

You did, too!

He looks around the room. His eyes stop on me, and I look out the window.

Please, Maddie, say something. Speak!

"Mr. Stoker?" Maddie calls out.

I've never been so happy to hear her voice. Did my brain send a telepathic message? This is a new skill.

"Yes?"

"May I go to the bathroom?"

"Yes, Maddie." Mr. Stoker adjusts the overhead. "Moving on...."

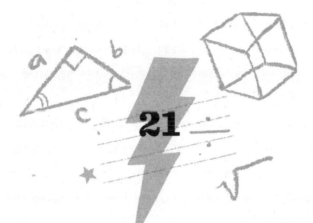

21

Saturday morning I pull out the numbers I've collected for the Pet Hut. I don't have enough data to do any real calculations. I need to go back.

I call Windy 1st to ask her to go with me.

"I can't. It's my dad's weekend. I have to hang out with him and his new girlfriend." She makes a gagging noise into the phone.

Next, I call Levi. I try not to think too much about it. I've never called a boy before and asked him to hang out or work on a project or anything. He might take it the wrong way, since Windy won't be there. And that's the last thing I want.

"Really? Windy's not going?" he asks, even though I've already told him that.

"Really. She's at her dad's this weekend."

"Then I'm in. But I need a ride."

"I'll take care of it. But no camera, okay?" I don't know the exact number (and that drives me crazy), but I know Levi has taken at least 17 pictures of me. He's also snapped 11 of Windy.

"That's like asking me *not* to bring my right arm."

Nana's way too happy when I ask her for a ride. She suggests I change my shirt and offers to curl my hair. I probably should have warned Levi. I probably should have canceled.

"I can't believe I'm driving my only granddaughter and a boy." She slaps the steering wheel as we head to his house. "Wait until I tell your uncle Paul."

"Please don't." I can already imagine the lecture he'd give me about boys and dating. And this is not a date!

"I knew middle school would be good for you."

"Nana, stop," I warn her.

"I know, I know, you're just friends."

"We're not even friends," I say. "We're partners on a project."

She turns to me and smiles wide. "And that's why you're wearing your hair down." She takes a strand in her fingers. "So pretty."

"It's because it's wet." I take the rubber band off my wrist and yank my hair into a ponytail.

Nana pulls into the driveway. Levi lives in a small, neat white house that's decorated with purple flowers and large pumpkins. It belongs on the cover of a real estate magazine.

"You want me to beep the horn, or are you going to ring the doorbell?" she asks.

"Don't beep." I get out of the car, hoping Levi will appear before I get to the door. He doesn't. Dogs bark from inside. I tap my toe 3 times and use my elbow to ring the doorbell.

Levi looks through the blinds before opening the door. I step back in case his killer guard dogs charge. But there's only a woman standing behind him.

"Hey," he says.

"Hey."

"Hi, Lucy. I'm Gina. Nice to meet you." She tilts her head and smiles when she talks. Gina has brown skin and black hair, like Levi. But his hair is curly on top, and her hair is supershort—almost like Uncle Paul's military haircut. She's wearing shorts, a tank top, and sneakers and is kind of sweaty. She's tall and skinny and probably could be a model. Levi is tall and skinny, too, but he has at least 6 inches to go to catch up with her.

"Nice to meet you." I wonder if Gina is his biological

mom and what his other mom looks like. And who is his biological dad? Seems rude to ask—or even think about. Something Windy would have no problem bringing up.

I hear the car door close and turn to see Nana coming up the sidewalk.

"Hello," she says as she steps onto the porch. "I'm Lucy's nana, Barb." She offers her hand to Gina.

"Hi. I'm Gina. Levi's mother."

Nana holds her hand out to Levi next. "Hi, Levi."

"It's nice to meet you, ma'am."

She turns to me and says, "What a polite young man." I give her a warning look, begging her not to say anything else.

"Thank you for driving them," Gina says. "I'm teaching a cardio class at 11 and another at 1. I could pick them up later."

"Don't worry about it," Nana says. "I'm happy to do it." I cringe, waiting for her to say something about my lack of a social life, but thankfully she's quiet.

Levi's mom kisses his cheek and says good-bye. I can't tell if he's embarrassed, because I look away.

We follow Nana back to the car. Levi gets in the back seat. I get in the front, taking my standard 3 tries to sit.

I usually don't like Nana's fast driving, but today I want her to push the car to its limits. Luckily, she keeps the conversation polite, and Levi doesn't look too uncomfortable.

"I remember when this used to be a Pizza Hut," Nana says as she stops in front of the shelter. "What time do you want me to pick you up?"

"They close at 5," I say.

"We're staying all day?" Levi asks.

"I am."

He groans.

Noah's behind the counter again. He's talking to a family and waves to Levi and me as we drop off our volunteer permission forms.

"We will be in the office," I say, like we're old co-workers.

Levi holds the door for me. The dogs bark and jump inside their kennels. As we walk past, I look around for Cutie Pi but don't see him.

We knock on the office door that's marked EMPLOY-EES ONLY. No one answers, so Levi opens it. All the papers are still on the desk. No one's touched anything since we were here last time. I sit, stand, sit, stand, sit in the chair.

"What am I supposed to do?" Levi asks.

"You can help me enter these into the computer," I say, patting the pile.

"No thanks."

"You could—"

Something under the desk brushes against my leg. I shove back in the chair and knock into the metal cabinets.

"What's wrong?" he asks.

"There is something under there!" I point. Whatever tried to snap off my leg is hidden in the shadows. My heart is thumping like when we ran the mile in gym class.

Levi rushes around the desk and drops to his knees. "It's Cutie Pi!"

I relax. Slightly.

"Here, boy." Levi lures him out with kissy sounds. The dog is shaking and keeps his tail between his back legs. I know how he feels.

"Now you have something to do." I motion to Cutie Pi with my head. "Get him out of here."

"Hey, Cutie Pi. Do you want to go for a walk?" Levi asks in a fake deep voice. "It sounds like I'm hitting on him."

"Maybe we should call him Pi," I suggest.

I double-check to make sure there's nothing else living under the desk. Then I turn on the computer.

Claire comes in as I'm wiping the keyboard with Clorox.

"I heard you were here," she says. "Thanks for coming in."

"Can I take Pi for a walk?" Levi asks. The dog hides behind Levi's legs. It's hard to imagine he would enjoy a walk.

"Sure. But keep him away from the other dogs. We don't have a vaccination record yet."

Pi tilts his head like he is trying to understand what's happening.

"Come on. It's okay," Levi assures the dog.

With Levi gone, Claire explains to me how to put the data into the computer. They use an old program that is similar to an address book.

"It's pretty simple," Claire says. She isn't kidding. There are better ways to track the information, but this will work for now.

I enter adoption form after adoption form into Claire's system. I also take the information I need and scribble it on a pad of paper. I could put it in a spreadsheet, but that would take away some of the fun. I collect each dog's breed, age, color, weight, and gender, and the number of days it took to be adopted. Since the Pet Hut is a no-kill shelter, all the animals are eventually adopted. Including Barnaby, a dog that lived here for 103 days before finding a home. He might still be here if some anonymous donor hadn't paid his $175 adoption fee. I don't bother working on the cats. I'm only interested in the dogs for now.

I work for 72 minutes before Levi and Pi finally come back.

"How's it going?" Levi unclips Pi's leash. The dog immediately pushes his way back under the desk.

"Fine." I don't want to be interrupted. Things are coming together. Correlation and causality. Things are making sense. I scribble another ratio on the pad of paper.

"What's that?" Levi asks.

"Nothing." I flip over the paper and send a pile of adoption forms sailing to the floor.

Levi snatches the pad of paper. "Looks like math. Like hard, gross math."

"Hey!" I jump up. My chair slides back into a filing cabinet. "Give me that."

"What are you working on?" He studies the sheet like he needs glasses. I grab for it, but Levi's faster.

"Come on!"

"Tell me what you're doing." He holds the pad over his head, teasing me. I jump. I miss. I jump. I miss. Of course, I feel the need to try a 3rd time and fail again. I'm so angry my arms shake.

"Levi!" My voice cracks.

"I'm just playing—"

Barking erupts from between us before Levi can finish his thought. Pi growls at Levi. The fur on his back sticks up. All his teeth are showing.

"Whoa." Levi steps back. He holds his hands out.

Pi quiets and walks to my right side. He sits, practically on my foot, and leans all his weight against my leg. I try to slide away, but Pi adjusts so he's still touching me. Gross.

"I'm sorry," Levi whispers.

"What got into the dog?" I imagine he's got a trigger

word that sets him off. I don't want to make him mad like Levi did.

"I think he likes you."

That doesn't make any sense. And the feeling is not mutual. "What do I do?"

"Pet him."

"No." I look down at the stupid dog. He looks up, his head tilted. Our eyes meet in a corny cartoon way. He does have beautiful brown eyes that are thoughtful and sad. Not that I'd tell him that. Not that he understands English.

"Pet him," Levi says again.

Pi's tail thwacks the floor with a beat.

1-2-3-4.

1-2-3-4.

1-2-3-4.

"Lucy, rub his head. Scratch him behind the ears."

"But dogs are so dirty."

"You don't have to lick him. Just pet him."

Since both Levi and Pi seem determined for this to happen, I lower my right hand and, with the tips of my fingers, stroke Pi's head 3 times. His eyes close. He pushes his head into my knee. These jeans are going right in the wash when I get home.

"You're a good dog," I say. I pet him some more, and I lose count of the number of times my hand moves back and forth.

"Here." Levi hands me my paper with the calculations. "I don't want your guard dog to attack again."

"He didn't attack. He gave you a warning."

Levi sits on the edge of the desk. "Are you going to tell me what you're doing or not?"

"It's statistics." I squirt hand sanitizer in my palm and then walk around to Levi. My new sidekick follows me. "I'm working on a formula. There's a pattern to how quickly a dog will be adopted. Like small dogs are adopted 1.75 times as fast as big dogs. Gray dogs find homes 2.2 times as quickly as black dogs. Dogs over the age of 8 take an average of 25 days to be adopted, which is over 2 times the average for all Pet Hut dogs. But this is all very preliminary. I need more numbers." When I sit, stand, sit, stand, sit in the chair, Pi watches with his head tilted.

"How did you come up with all this?" Levi asks.

"It's not that hard for me." I drop the pad on the desk. Across the sheet are averages and standard deviations for the 107 dogs most recently adopted.

"I hate math." His upper lip curls in disgust. "It bites. Math hates me, and I hate math."

"I could help you," I offer. "I'm kind of good with numbers."

"Will you do my homework?"

"No."

He picks up my calculations again and flips through the 4 pages. His eyes narrow. He shakes his head slightly.

"How good are you?" he asks.

"Really good." Pi pushes his way back under the desk. I look at him instead of Levi.

"Really good?" He does air quotes around *really good.* "Don't make me sing 'liar, liar, pants on fire.' I hate to sing."

"Fine. I'm freaky-excellent-genius-good at math."

"Seems you're good with adjectives, too."

I take a deep breath and tell him my story before I lose my nerve. I want someone to understand that I might not be normal, but this—the numbers, the OCD—is my normal.

"When I was 8 years old, I was struck by lightning. Part of my brain was injured, and I ended up with super number abilities."

Levi's eyes open wide. "Seriously?"

I can tell he doesn't believe me. So I try to dazzle him by reciting pi to the 314th digit.

"I don't know if you're right," he says.

"Trust me. I am." Then I hand him the oversized plastic calculator Claire keeps on the desk. I tell him to quiz me. I add, subtract, multiply, divide all the numbers he throws at me. We play this game for over 10 minutes, which is plenty of time for me to worry that I've made a huge mistake in telling him my secret.

"Enough," I finally say.

"You're a freak." He smiles, exposing the gap between his front teeth.

I shrug. I already knew that. "Don't tell anyone. Okay?"

"Cross my heart and hope to die. Do you need me to pinkie-promise, too?" Which is his way of promising to keep quiet and sort of mocking me at the same time.

"And I was serious. If you ever need help with math, I could tutor you," I offer.

"Gee, thanks, Mighty Math Genius."

"Actually, I prefer Lightning Girl." I touch my necklace. "And you can always go online if you don't want to be seen with me." I tell him about the MathWhiz website.

"Why wouldn't I want to be seen with you?"

I shrug again. I'm not sure why I said that. The small office suddenly feels too warm.

"So, do you want to help me enter this stuff?" I ask.

"I don't know if I'm qualified, Lightning Girl."

"I'm qualified enough for both of us." I point to the pile of forms on the floor. We spend the rest of the day entering adoption information into the computer and collecting my own sampling. A scraggly dog sleeps on my feet. Levi complains the whole time. It might be the best afternoon of my life.

I can't explain it, but I trust that Levi will keep my secret. Unlike Windy, he rarely talks about other people. I know I should get it over with and tell her, too. She's my best friend, and she shares every detail of her life with me. Like last night, she told me about the time she peed her pants waiting in line for a roller coaster. And it wasn't a story from when she was 5. It happened last year. I'd want to forget something like that, not admit it. The problem is, she also tells me about everyone else. From her mom—who needs to wax a mustache—to which kids repeated kindergarten. There's no controlling information once it's in Windy's head. No vault. No lock and key. No secret combination.

I'm also worried she might be hurt that I'm keeping something from her.

Luckily, Windy and I have plenty of other stuff to talk about, like the musical *Wicked* (her newest favorite), her birthday party, and global warming. She watched a video with a starving polar bear last weekend, and the next day she insisted on walking to school. She only made it about ¾ of a mile—just to the next bus stop.

It takes me 2 more visits to the Pet Hut to finish entering all the data into the computer and collecting it for my own purposes. Levi and Windy join me on Monday. They play with dogs while I stay in the office. Wednesday, I go alone to complete my work. The numbers are fascinating. I share them with SquareHead314 and Numberlicious, but they aren't impressed. They say my sample of 242 dogs isn't large enough to make any definite conclusions. But it's not like I'm going to go to another animal shelter to collect more data.

I don't visit the Pet Hut *just* for the numbers. I also like to see Pi. He still doesn't have a kennel to call his own. So I try to make his under-the-desk doghouse more comfortable. I bring him an old sweatshirt to sleep on. It's green and yellow (like the numbers 14 and 102) and too small for me. But while I'm working on the computer, he prefers to sleep on my lap, which is gross and adorable.

I think our Cougar Cares Project is going great. If it were up to me, I'd even say we've done enough; their adoption files are all digital and up to date. We can keep visiting the Pet Hut to enter any new paperwork—and to check on Pi. But Windy still wants to make a difference. On Thursday night, we have a group phone call to see how we can change the world. Our revised project plan is due tomorrow.

"Okay, guys. What are we going to do?" Windy asks, in charge as always. "We need some good ideas, like right now."

"Let's just have a bake sale, raise some money, and get it over with," Levi says.

"Do you bake?" I lie back on my bed.

"No."

"Think bigger," Windy demands.

"A big bake sale," Levi says.

Windy groans. "I'm so glad this isn't for a grade, or I'd kick your butt out of this group."

I can imagine Levi smiling at his end. He likes to get Windy upset. And he's good at it.

"Maybe we could have a bake sale for pets," I say. "We can make homemade dog treats and grow catnip. People who love animals will come to the sale. We'll raise funds and maybe get people to adopt another pet."

"Will you 2 give up on the bake sale?" Windy says. "Besides, we can't raise money. They told us that on the 1st day."

"Lucy, tell us what you've been working on," Levi

says. "I see you scribbling your … your ideas down." He doesn't say *formula* or *equation* or *math*. I guess he's trying to keep my secret.

"What's he talking about?" Windy's voice cracks. I can't tell whether she's hurt or mad.

"As I was entering the adoption information into the computers, I just noticed some interesting things. That's all." I tell her what I told Levi last weekend. "Certain types of dogs take longer to get adopted. Pit bulls take 19 days to be adopted, while terriers take only 8."

"How did you figure that out?" Windy asks.

"It's not like it's hard," Levi says, covering for me. "Even I can calculate an average."

"So what? How does this help us?" Windy says.

"Um, that doesn't seem fair," I say.

"Maybe we could change those odds," Levi offers. "My mom runs a marketing firm. People come to her to get more business or get more attention. Like she helps new restaurants get reviews and sends out coupons. The unpopular dogs need a publicist." I get the feeling that the idea didn't just pop into his head.

"So, what do you suggest?" Windy asks.

"The Pet Hut website is beyond pathetic," Levi says.

"You want to redesign their website?" Windy asks. I can imagine her lip curled in disgust.

"I want to get dogs adopted," he says.

I log on to my computer and go to the Pet Hut website. It has the basic information about adoption fees and the shelter's hours. There are a few pictures and a very out-of-date blog. The last post was 67 days ago. It's a success story about a poodle mix that was adopted and lives with a family. I click around some more. The site doesn't have any posts about animals waiting to be adopted.

"Lucy! Lucy!" Windy yells. "Are you there?"

"I'm here."

"Lucy, how long does it usually take a dog to get adopted?" Levi asks.

"The average wait time for all dogs is 12 days. Not counting puppies."

"So the goal is to lower that number, and we do that by focusing on the dogs that take a superlong time to get adopted," Windy says. "We'll put them on the website. We can write feature articles on them." We've done feature articles in language arts class. We had to write about a famous dead author.

"I'm not writing anything," Levi says. "I'll take pictures."

"That's a good idea. And I'll figure out which dogs need our help the most." I don't want to write, either.

"This is awesome, guys. We're going to save thousands of puppies."

"No puppies. They don't need help finding homes."

According to my math, dogs under 6 months old are adopted within 3 days.

"Fine," Windy says. "We're going to save thousands of dogs."

"Or 10," I say, trying to keep Windy from expecting too much.

23

Some teachers can't be trusted. I thought Ms. Fleming and I had an understanding. For 4 weeks, she's been giving me the class readings to look over ahead of time—3 short stories and our 1st assigned novel, *The Call of the Wild*. She thinks I'm prereading the stuff, but all I really need to do is count the words. Then when she calls on me in class, I have no problem reading aloud.

Today, she breaks that fragile trust we've built. And I know it's no accident. She asks Maddie and Jennifer to hand out the anthologies. I haven't counted any words in this book.

"When you get your book, turn to page 97," Ms.

Fleming says to the whole class, but her eyes are focused on me.

I don't have my book yet. I need to start counting. My face grows hot as I wait. Maddie finally gets to me. She coughs on the cover before dropping the book onto my desk. I use the sleeve of my sweatshirt to open it.

The text is dense. It's the abridged version of *The Odyssey*.

"Lucy, why don't you start?"

I haven't even tallied a single word yet.

"I can't. My throat." I rub my neck.

"Just give it a try." She looks down at the podium, where her book sits. *What kind of middle school teacher needs a podium?*

"No."

"No?"

"No."

She does that thing where she takes off her glasses and puts 1 of the end pieces to her lips.

I close my book and cross my arms over my stomach. I'm not acting. I might throw up.

"I'll read," Windy offers, like she did the 1st week of school.

"No, Windy. I told Lucy to read." Ms. Fleming steps in front of her podium. "Read the 1st page, Lucy. You can do this. You've been working really hard."

"I can't." My eyes are cloudy.

"Now, Miss Callahan."

"Leave her alone," Windy says. "Look at her. She's sick. Or about to be."

"You are both dangerously close." She holds her fingers about a ½ inch, maybe ¾ inch, apart. But I'm not sure what she's measuring.

Windy mutters something and shakes her head.

"Lucy Callahan, this is the last time I'm asking," Ms. Fleming says.

"You aren't really asking," someone interrupts.

It's not Windy this time. It's Levi.

"You're demanding. She doesn't want to read. Leave her alone." He's slumped in his chair, and it looks like he's talking to the textbook.

"You're being a bully," Windy adds.

And that's all it takes for Ms. Fleming to finally snap. "Get out of my classroom!"

Levi gets up 1st and grabs his bag. I follow him, slipping the anthology under my binder. I'm taking it home to count the words later.

Windy is sickly pale and frozen in her seat. "I'm sorry."

"Go." Ms. Fleming squeezes her glasses. They bend but don't break.

"Come on, Windy. Take 1 for the team." Levi holds the door open for us. When I get in the hall, I tap my toe 3 times.

Windy's right behind us. Her eyes are wet.

"You didn't have to do that," I say, and hand her a wrapped Clorox wipe because I don't carry tissues.

"I know." She sniffs hard and wipes her eyes on her sleeve.

"What do we do now?" I ask.

"I don't know. I've never been in trouble," Windy says, and more tears drop.

"I guess we should go to the main office," Levi suggests.

We tell the secretary we've been kicked out of Ms. Fleming's language arts class for not reading aloud. She tells us to take a seat. We wait the rest of the period for Dr. Cobb, but it turns out he doesn't have time for us. When the bell rings, we're sent on to 4th period.

The rest of the day continues without incident. But I notice that Windy keeps looking at the door like she expects security forces to come busting through. Even on the bus ride home, she's still worried that her perfect record is tarnished.

"Thanks for, ya know . . . ," I tell her as she gets off.

Windy nods. It's obvious she regrets the stand she took for me. Maybe there's a way I can make it up to her. But Twizzlers and gummy bears don't seem like enough of a gesture.

When I get home, Nana is waiting on the couch, and the TV isn't on. Maybe the school called and told her that I got kicked out of language arts class.

"Hey. Is everything okay?" I ask as I help myself to hand sanitizer.

"Lucy, I've got some good news."

I drop my backpack and sit, stand, sit, stand, sit on the living room chair. "What?"

"I was waiting on a family this morning, and the credit card machine was taking its sweet time. The son—he looked to be 16—wore a sweatshirt that said NCASME, and it had some math symbols on it and a microscope. I asked him what it stood for."

She pauses like I should fill in this part of her story.

"North Carolina Academy of Science, Math, and Engineering," she says. "It's a special high school for juniors and seniors. They do all subjects, but the focus is math. And it's free because it's a public school. The students live in dorms and have meals in the cafeteria. It's all free."

"That's cool."

"And the boy. His name is Paul. Paul! This is a sign, Lucy."

"It is? Just because this stranger shares a name with my uncle and goes to a math school, that doesn't really feel like a major sign. Maybe if his name was Lucy."

She ignored me. "And Paul said there is a girl at the school who is only 13. Isn't that amazing?"

I nod. "Is her name Lucy?"

"I've no clue." Nana throws up her hands.

"Because that would be more of a sign."

"Stop being silly. This school is perfect. You can be around other smart kids. It's not college, and it's not middle school. I've called the admissions office to see how we can get you in."

"Where is it?"

"Near Charlotte."

"Charlotte's almost 2 hours away."

Nana tilts her head. She reminds me of Pi. "I thought you'd be more excited. I even got Paul's email and phone number so you can ask him questions. You're made for this school, Lucy."

"Okay."

"What's wrong?"

"Nothing."

Nana claps her hands once and stands up. "I'm going to call the admissions office again."

It's weird. Ms. Fleming's class today was the 1st time I felt like I belonged at East Hamlin. And it wasn't because of Ms. Fleming—that's for sure. Windy and Levi made the difference. No one has ever helped me out like that before. *I've* never helped anyone else like that. It's different from assisting with math homework online. They could have gotten in real trouble. They might still.

∞

The next day, we return to Ms. Fleming's class. There's no mention of our revolt. No apologies from us or from her. It's like everyone is trying to forget it happened. Except I know Ms. Fleming hasn't forgotten, because she doesn't ask me to read a single word. I guess I wasted 2 hours last night counting every word in that stupid anthology book.

"Looks like we got away with it," Levi whispers.

"I hope so," Windy says.

I smile but say nothing. I'm not sure how all this works. Do I thank them? Do I owe them? Words and favors don't seem like enough. They saved me in more ways than 1.

24

Last week, Mr. Stoker liked our idea of writing a blog post about pets that need a home. He gave us a thumbs-up and an encouraging "I knew you'd come up with something smart." On the 2nd Wednesday in October we get out of school 2 hours early for a teacher-work day, and Cherish drives us back to the Pet Hut to meet with Claire.

"This is a great idea," Claire says for the 4th time. She probably would have been enthusiastic if we'd offered to make mittens for the animals. She's good at making volunteers feel important.

"Thank you," Windy says. "We're soooo excited about this."

"Are you going to do it on our website?" she asks.

"If that's okay," Levi says.

"Yeah. Sure, sure. This is really a great idea." 5th time! "And I know exactly which animal you should feature 1st."

"No, that's Lucy's job," Windy says. "She has a theory."

Claire raises her eyebrows. "Really?"

"Do you mind?" I ask.

"Not at all. I'll take any help I can get." She motions to the room of dog kennels.

Levi opens the door for me, probably just a habit. I take out my notebook with my formula. I know big dogs are harder to adopt (except for Chihuahuas), so I focus on the animals in the 8 kennels on the floor. My formula has variables for age, color, breed, and size.

I walk by each kennel and read the attached clipboard to get the information I need. Claire, Levi, and Windy follow me quietly, like they don't want to break my concentration. But the math is actually very simple. I don't even need to write anything down.

The average wait time to be adopted is 12 days. So my formula starts with that, and I add or subtract based on the data I've collected.

If the breed is pit bull, I add 7 to the 12 days; a shepherd gets plus 4 days, and a Chihuahua gets 2 extra days. No other breed falls outside the standard deviation. Basically, they all get a plus 0.

For weight, big dogs (over 60 pounds) get a 2-day add.

And 5 days are added for a black coat. No other coloring played a major factor in my calculations.

Age has 2 criteria: If the dog is between 3 and 7 years old, I add 3 days. And if the animal is over 8 years old, I add a whopping 10 days.

There's only 1 situation where I need to subtract any days. A dog less than 1 year old gets minus 4 days.

"What is all that in your notebook?" Windy asks.

I close it. "Just some thoughts. Where's Pi?" I ask, hoping Windy won't ask more questions.

"He's at the vet," Claire says. "He needs exams and vaccinations before he'll be ready for adoption."

That makes sense. According to my calculations, Pi wouldn't have been my chosen dog anyway. I walk back to the 2nd kennel.

"This dog." I point at the 110-pound, 6-year-old shepherd mix with mostly black fur and mismatched eyes. I don't have a variable for eye color, but I bet his uniqueness would scare some people.

12 days + 4 days (shepherd mix) + 2 days (weight) + 3 days (age) + 5 days (black) = 26 days

"He got here 2 days ago," Claire says.

I shrug. "I have a feeling he'll need help finding a home." It's not a feeling. It's a calculation. According to my math model, he will take 24 to 28 days to be adopted. That's longer than any other dog that is currently here. The Lab mix in kennel 8 has been at the shelter the longest, 18 days, but should be adopted between 16 and 20 days. Or any day now. Pi should be between 11 and 15.

"All right." Claire shrugs. "Let's take him to the play yard in the back. You can get to know Murphy."

"This is going to be awesome," Windy says. And Levi doesn't even disagree with her.

The moment Claire opens the kennel door, Murphy transforms from quiet and still to loud and excited. She gives him an awkward bear hug while Levi slips a harness and leash on him.

"Thanks," Claire says. "Wait. Y'all filled out your volunteer forms, right?" She laughs, but I think she's being serious. This dog looks ready to maul someone.

"Yep," Windy answers for all of us.

Murphy jumps up. His paws land on Claire's shoulders. She nudges him off with an elbow and a knee. Maybe math shouldn't be the only consideration when picking a dog to rescue.

"Lucy, you look nervous," Claire says.

"I'm okay." I fiddle with my lightning-bolt charm.

Murphy pulls against the leash. Claire has no choice but to follow him down the hall. Luckily, he's heading in the right direction.

The play yard doesn't have much to play with except a chewed tennis ball. It's surrounded by a tall chain link fence. The ground is a concrete pad. A weatherworn wooden bench (that also has teeth marks notched out of the legs) sits along the side.

Claire closes the gate behind us. I feel trapped because I am. I tap my toe 3 times.

"Where did he come from?" Windy asks.

"He was surrendered. An older woman was raising him," Claire answers. "She lived in an apartment, and her husband died suddenly. She couldn't handle the dog on her own. Bless her heart."

"You poor thing," Windy says, nuzzling the dog.

"I'll be right over there. Holler if you need me." Claire locks us in.

"Maybe I should see if there are new adoption forms that need to be entered into the computer." I turn to the gate, ready to run. Dogs are gross and coated in bacteria and parasites—so are humans. But dogs also bite and maul, and they sense fear. They're practically mind readers. To Murphy, I probably appear to be a trembling chew toy.

"Stay," Levi says. "He won't hurt you. I won't let him. I promise."

Feeling wanted beats feeling safe. So I stay.

Levi takes off Murphy's harness. The dog jumps from corner to corner, like he's playing tag with invisible friends.

"I know what we need to write about this dog," Windy says. "Brain-damaged."

"He is not," Levi says.

I try not to let the brain damage comment sting. But it does a little.

"He's never going to sit still for a picture," Windy says. She keeps patting her leg trying to get him to come to her.

"Murphy's just excited. Give him a minute to calm down." Levi hangs his backpack on the fence post. He takes out his camera and a bow tie and a fedora.

"Are we playing dress-up?" Windy asks.

The dog tries to snatch the hat from Levi's hand. I gasp and jump on the bench. "Maybe I should go. I'm making him nervous."

"Since you're up there, you can hold the backdrop." Levi hands me a blue-green sheet (the color of the number 15), and we all wait for Murphy to relax. He finally lets Windy pet his head.

"Good dog." It takes Levi 3 tries to get the bow tie on. Murphy doesn't care for the hat at all.

Windy backs out of the shot. Levi gets down on his knees to take the picture while I hold the sheet. The dog looks everywhere except at Levi until Windy picks up the ratty tennis ball. She bounces it once. Murphy is mesmerized. Then Windy holds the ball next to Levi's head. I'm worried for Levi's safety. I'm not a good judge of dogs, but based on Murphy's drooling and intense focus, I'd guess he'd do anything—including decapitating my teammates—to get to that ball.

"Got it," Levi says.

Murphy is rewarded with attention from Levi, who rubs his belly, and the tennis ball from Windy.

After Claire comes back to get Murphy, she lets us use the office to work on our 1st blog post. Windy does the typing. Eventually, we get down a description of Murphy, and Levi figures out how to upload the pictures. Claire reads the post and declares it perfect. Then she gives Windy and Levi a hug. I slide out of the way to avoid contact.

As we leave, I give Murphy a thumbs-up. "I hope the math is good to you, boy."

25

Only 27 hours after our post about Murphy goes up, he's adopted. Windy acts like we saved the last black rhino from extinction.

"Calm down," Levi warns her before homeroom. "We've helped 1 dog find a home. And Murphy only got adopted so quick because my mom put links to the Pet Hut blog all over her social media."

"We saved a life." Windy sits on Levi's desk, her legs swinging back and forth.

"It's a no-kill shelter," he reminds her.

Windy shrugs. "Still. Without us, who knows how long poor Murphy would have suffered in that place?"

"He wasn't suffering," Levi says.

"Ugh," Maddie moans as she walks by. "We're all suffering just listening to you 3."

"Then don't listen," Levi shoots back.

"And I looked at your website," Maddie says.

"It's a blog," Windy corrects her.

"Whatever," Maddie continues. "You had about 100 spelling mistakes, and you also—"

"Cool!" Levi says. "I'm glad you checked it out. Nice to know you're a fan."

Maddie does an exaggerated shiver. "I'm not." She hesitates like she has more to say, but she doesn't. She rolls her eyes and walks over to Daniela.

"Anyway," Windy says, "we need to go back tonight and pick another dog. I'll get Cherish to drive us after school." She pulls out her phone to text her sister.

"I can't," I tell her.

"Why?" Windy asks.

"I have an appointment." An appointment I don't want to go to. Nana's arranged an interview and a tour of NCASME—the high school for supersmart math-and-science-loving students.

"What appointment? Doctor? Dentist? Ortho?" Windy asks. "Are you getting braces?"

"You don't need to know everything," Levi says. "If Lucy wants you to know, she'll tell you."

Windy sticks out her bottom lip. She's pretending to be hurt. Or maybe she actually is a little bit hurt.

Mr. Stoker claps his hands twice. "You have less than a minute before the bell. Please find your seats."

"Levi, you can still go, right?" Windy asks as she gets up.

"I guess. But I'm only doing it for the dogs. Not for you."

Windy smiles. "Whatever." She shrugs and walks off.

When I know she's out of hearing range, I lean toward Levi. "Hey. Were you on MathWhiz last night?" I assume it was him. The username was Levi123.

He nods.

"Did you get all your questions answered?"

"Yeah, Lightning Girl. I did." He takes out his homework and holds it up. "See."

"Okay. Let me know if you need ..." I don't finish my sentence.

"I will"

∞

Nana and Uncle Paul pick me up at 12. He's only in town for 2 days, and I can't believe this is how he wants to spend his afternoon.

The ride to the academy takes 103 minutes, 14 left turns, 22 right turns, and 5 times of Nana telling me not to be nervous. After the 1st time, her words have the opposite effect.

"You got this, genius," Uncle Paul says as we get out of the car.

We follow Nana into a pretty white house with blue shutters (like the number 7). I would think it's just a house except it has a sign in the yard that says ADMISSIONS.

"Don't be nervous," Nana says again.

We wait for our appointment in the living room. Uncle Paul points out all the science magazines perfectly arranged on the table. "They couldn't throw in 1 *Sports Illustrated*. What do they have against basketball and football? And what about boxing? Did you know that's called the sweet science?"

"Why?" I ask.

"I got no idea."

A woman wearing gray pants (kind of like the number 99) and a sweater with the NCASME logo invites us into her office. She introduces herself as Cheryl McCleary, but she doesn't say if I should call her Cheryl or Ms. McCleary.

"Have a seat," she says.

I sit. And I don't get up. Nana pats my knee like she's impressed. It doesn't last.

3.141592 . . .

I stand. I sit. I stand. I sit. The numbers retreat.

Ms. McCleary doesn't say anything about the OCD dance—most adults don't—but she's also good at hiding her surprise. Maybe she's met kids like me before—other students who have obsessive routines and patterns. I want to ask her but can't think of a polite way to do so.

"Lucy, thank you for coming to visit our school," Ms. McCleary begins. "We're honored to have you consider us for your education."

"Thanks." I wish I knew whether she says this to every student.

"I've reviewed your homeschool records and your achievement tests. They're all very impressive. We don't have any grades from East Hamlin Middle yet." She pats the folder on her desk.

"Middle school has been a bit of an adjustment," Nana says.

"Isn't it for everybody?" Uncle Paul adds.

"It certainly can be. Students thrive in different environments. You can't expect a rose to bloom in the desert. But put the rose in a greenhouse with sunlight and water, it will blossom."

Ms. McCleary stares at us, hoping we get the point. I give a slight nod.

"I love roses," Nana blurts out.

"Me too," Ms. McCleary says with a smile. "Lucy, do you need to use the bathroom or would you like a drink before you begin the exam?"

"What exam?" I slide my lightning-bolt charm back and forth on its chain.

"They want to see if you're smart enough," Nana says with a wink. She obviously knew about this part of the *tour* but didn't bother to warn me.

"You ace every test," Uncle Paul says. "Nothing to worry about."

"It's our standard entrance exam," Ms. McCleary adds. "It's required of all students who do not come from traditional schools. It's 150 questions. All multiple-choice. Half are mathematics, and the rest are science, vocabulary, and social studies. You have 2 hours to complete it. So, do you need a restroom break?"

"No." I look over at Nana. Her eyes are closed and her lips are moving. She's praying. I guess she really wants me to do well.

Ms. McCleary shows me to a conference room. The test booklet, 2 pencils, and scrap paper wait for me on the table. Nana and Uncle Paul stay in her office. I wonder what they'll do while I answer 150 multiple-choice questions.

I open a Clorox wipe and clean the table and pencils. Again, Ms. McCleary acts like this is totally normal.

"Do you need anything else?" She holds out her hand for the used wipe.

"No, thank you."

"Good luck," she says.

In general, I don't mind tests. I find them boring but not scary. Some kids panic. Spencer, the boy who sits next to me in science, panics. When we have a test, I can hear his breathing get fast. His leg bounces nonstop. And when he lifts his arms, he smells sweaty.

I open the booklet. I look at my watch. I answer all the math questions. I look at my watch again. 11 minutes have passed. The rest of the test takes me less than an hour. About half of that time is spent counting the words. I'm sure I get every question right. I debate going back and changing a few answers, but at this school, getting them all correct is probably the average. Not hiding my genius is like taking off a pair of sweaty old sneakers. It feels good now, but I don't think I'm ready to toss my sneakers.

After the test, Ms. McCleary gives us a tour. It's hard not to be impressed by the science labs with shiny equipment, or the 3-D printers in the classrooms, or the music room where I could learn to play the harp, or the coffee bar in the student center. Windy would love a coffee bar.

"Obviously, we aren't your typical high school. We only cover 11th and 12th grades. We have a 100 percent graduation rate. All of our students go to college, and 92 percent receive at least partial scholarships."

"This is an awesome school," Uncle Paul whispers to me. "Do you think I'm too old to apply? Or just too dumb?"

I elbow him in the gut.

"This way." We follow Ms. McCleary back to her office. A basket with Oreos, Pringles, and oranges sits on her desk, along with 4 bottles of water and 4 cans of Coke.

"Help yourself."

I go for the Oreos. I'm opening the package when my phone chimes in my jacket pocket.

"Sorry. I'll silence it."

"No worries. I have 2 teenage daughters," Ms. McCleary says. "I'll be right back."

When she leaves, I pull out my phone.

Windy: what dog should we pick

Windy: ???

"Is it an emergency, Doctor?" Nana asks, joking.

"To someone it is," I say.

Windy: Lucy! Help!

Me: kennel 4

Kennel 4 holds a dog named Rufus, a brown pit bull estimated to be 4 or 5 years old and weighing 60 pounds. I calculated his adoption time to be 22 to 26 days.

Windy: Rufus?

Me: yes

Me: unless there's a new dog over 8 years, black fur, weighing more than 60 pounds, and is mostly pit bull or shepherd

I wait for the response.

Windy: Nope

Me: any Chihuahuas?

Chihuahuas are the only non-large breed that I calculated with a high adoption wait. They make the formula interesting.

Windy: we r going with Rufus!

I should be there. If an old black Chihuahua is available, it's not fair to go with Rufus. (This theoretical dog is calculating at 29 to 33 days.) I chew on my bottom lip as I debate calling Levi.

"You okay?" Uncle Paul asks.

I nod.

"Boy problems?"

"No!"

When Ms. McCleary steps back into the room, Nana hits my arm. I silence my phone and put it away.

"Do you have any questions?" she asks.

Not really, plus my mouth is stuffed with Oreos.

"Does Lucy qualify?" Nana asks.

"She earned a perfect test score," Ms. McCleary says. "This is not unheard of, but still, it's very impressive. Now, Lucy will need to apply officially online."

"Okay," Nana says.

"I'd recommend you get this information in as soon as possible. Within the next few weeks, ideally. We are opening 2 spots for January. This is a great opportunity. We don't generally allow students to begin midyear."

January? That's only 81 days away.

"Lucky for you, Luce." Uncle Paul smiles. When I don't smile back at him, he mouths, *What?*

I shake my head.

"You have an excellent chance of being admitted." Ms. McCleary reaches into her desk, pulls out a cap with NCASME on it, and hands it to me.

I swallow the last of the Oreo. It goes down my throat like a baseball. I just started a new school. It was awful, and now it's not so awful. I don't know if I'm ready to do it all over again.

26

I haven't gone out on Halloween since my brain got rewired by lightning. I don't think 1 has anything to do with the other. I've never loved Halloween. It's a lot of effort to get candy, and we *always* have candy in our apartment anyway. The last time I dressed up, I was 7 and went as a hybrid Disney princess. I had Ariel's red hair and Belle's yellow gown. Nana said if I liked both, I didn't have to choose.

Windy, however, loves Halloween. And she's insisting that Levi and I go trick-or-treating in her neighborhood. I try to get out of it with the most logical excuse. "I don't have a costume," I tell her. She offers to lend me 1 of her old outfits. There's Cosette from *Les Mis*, or Eliza from

Hamilton, or Sophie from *Mamma Mia!* But Nana comes up with something I actually like.

"You look great," Nana says when I model for her in our living room.

I give her a salute. I'm wearing Uncle Paul's old fatigues (adjusted to my size with safety pins), his dog tags, and a cap. I've also painted my face camouflage. It's the 1st time I've ever worn makeup.

"Did you finish the NCASME application?" she asks.

"Yes, but I probably won't get in. I had to leave whole portions of it blank. I have no leadership experience. I've never been part of a team. And the only volunteer work I've done is tutoring math online." Which has gone from 30 hours a week to 10. (And most of that is spent helping and chatting with Levi123.)

"What about all this time you spend with dogs at the Pizza Hut?"

"That's required for school. It's an assigned project."

"Wouldn't hurt to have included it. You go there every other day," she says. "Now smile. I want to send a picture to Uncle Paul." After taking 4 photos with her cell phone, she drives me to Windy's. Levi is already there, waiting on the front porch. He's wearing a camera around his neck and a fedora with PRESS on a slip of paper tucked into the ribbon.

He takes my picture as I join him.

"Can we limit the number of pictures you take of me?" I ask, knowing he can't be stopped.

"That's like asking me not to breathe."

"No, it's not. It's like asking you not to take my picture."

"Sorry," he mumbles, and plays with the buttons on the back of the camera.

"It's okay," I say, feeling like a jerk. "Let's just keep it to single digits."

Cherish lets us in and tells us to wait in the living room. Windy's not quite ready.

"Bet she wants to make a big entrance." Levi takes a seat on the couch.

I sit, stand, sit, stand, sit on a chair across from him. Then I wonder if I should have sat next to him. Then I wonder why I'm wondering this. I shake my head to clear the thoughts.

Ms. Sitton has left out a veggie tray on the coffee table. I munch on a carrot stick.

"I stopped by the Pet Hut on my way here. Jesse had an adoption application already," Levi says. "We only put up her profile last night." We picked Jesse as our 7th dog to feature. She's a bulldog mix, with brown, black, and gray swirled coloring, probably close to 10 years old. (I estimate her adoption wait would be 22 to 26 days without our help. Unless we consider her swirly coat to be mostly black; then she'd average 27 to 31 days.) She's the kind of dog that's so ugly she's cute. It helped that Levi dressed her in a bonnet for the picture. Even I was tempted to touch her, but that might have made Pi jealous.

Strangely, Pi isn't up for adoption yet. He's becoming more of a Pet Hut mascot. He sleeps in the office, and when we come to visit—which has been 3 times in the last week—I keep him company while Windy and Levi get to know the other dogs. I've taught Pi to sit, lie down, and roll over. He's a very smart dog. I don't ask Claire why he hasn't been moved into a kennel, because I don't want him to leave. Which is selfish because I know I can't adopt him. Nana's not a dog person, and our lease doesn't allow pets. I actually dug out the document from Nana's file cabinet to double-check. *No pets allowed.*

"Guess we'll get to pick dog number 8 on Friday."

"Maybe we should do 2 dogs," Levi suggests.

"We could."

I help myself to more vegetables. I'd rather have a Snickers or a Twix, but Ms. Sitton is handing out scented pencils to trick-or-treaters.

"Levi, are you ready?" Windy shouts from the top of the stairs. "Get your camera."

Windy walks slowly down the 18 steps. She's wearing a white jumpsuit, a white hat, a mask over her mouth and nose, and orange rubber gloves (like the number 6).

"What are you supposed to be?" Levi asks.

"I'm a shrimp worker. I'm forced to shell shrimp for 18 hours a day for pennies in awful conditions. Here." She gives Levi and me a postcard that lists all the brands with abusive labor practices. "I'm handing these out as we go door to door," she explains. "But I still want candy. I'm just taking advantage of the holiday to help the oppressed."

"This should be fun," Levi says.

Windy's neighborhood is perfect for trick-or-treating. The houses are huge but close together, and most residents are home. I estimate my Walmart bag weighs 1 pound by the time we get to the end of her street.

"I'm going to have to hide this candy," Windy says. "My mom isn't going to let me keep all 1,000 pieces."

"29," I correct her.

"You've been counting?" she asks.

I shrug.

Windy stops and looks in the quilted pumpkin bag that has her name stitched on the front.

"I do have 29 pieces. How many do you have?"

"30. The last house gave Levi and me extra. I don't think they appreciated your shrimp postcards. But Levi only has 27 because he keeps eating his Whoppers."

"What?" He crunches his candy. "I love Whoppers."

"It's just weird. You're always counting stuff." She stands under a streetlight. "Is it part of your OCD?"

I tap my toe 3 times.

"Leave her alone." Levi opens another wrapper.

"I'm not picking on her." Windy pulls down her mask. "You're just really obsessed with numbers."

"I am," I admit.

Windy's quiet, which sends a little shiver from my toes to my neck. She's always talking, but right now she wants me to tell her more. I could keep walking. She doesn't need to know everything about me. But she's my friend—my best friend—and if I don't tell her now, then when? Is there ever a perfect time to reveal that you're a freak?

I take a breath and hold it, like I'm about to lift something heavy.

"I love numbers, and I love math. My brain is high-functioning when it comes to numbers. Um...actually, I'm a genius. A math genius."

She raises her eyebrows.

"When I was 8, I was struck by lightning. The electricity destroyed part of this side of my brain." I tap my left temple. "But this side was jolted awake. It's called acquired savant syndrome."

"Whoa. I had no idea," Levi jokes.

Windy shakes her head. "But I get better grades than you do. Even in math."

"I don't want people to know." I shrug. "I had a deal with my grandmother that I had to survive 1 year of middle school. I'm already the *cleaning lady*. I don't need to stick out any more."

A car drives by and blasts its horn. We step into the grass.

"But ..." Windy folds her arms across her chest. "But, I don't ..." She stares into the streetlight.

"But what?" I ask.

"I guess I don't get it," she says. "If I were a genius, I'd want the world to know."

"Lucy's not you," Levi says.

"I know that!" she snaps at him. Then she turns to me. "How much of a genius are you?"

My cheeks burn. How should I answer?

"Lucy, what's the circumference of a circle with a radius of 8 yards?" Levi asks.

"50.265 yards. Or 150.796 feet. Or 1,809.557 inches. Of course, I'm rounding to the thousandth place."

"And the area?" Levi asks.

"201.062 square yards."

"I guess you've been doing more than counting stuff," Windy says.

"Are you mad that I didn't tell you?" I ask Windy.

"I'm mad that I didn't notice. I should have noticed. Like with the dogs and the averages." She rubs her forehead.

"You kinda did." I try to make her feel better.

"Why didn't you tell me before?" Her eyes meet mine, and I feel guilty, or maybe scared, or maybe both.

I look away. "I don't know." There's no good way to say, *I was worried you'd blab to everyone.*

"Give her a break," Levi says, opening another box of candy. "She did tell you 2 minutes ago. Lucy's like a nervous teacup Chihuahua. She takes a while to trust someone."

I know Levi is trying to help. But I don't like being compared to a jittery dog.

"How long have you known?" Windy asks him.

"Longer than 2 minutes. But I'm like a golden retriever. Very trustworthy."

"Well, what kind of dog am I?" She looks at Levi.

"A mutt," I answer quickly. And they both stare at me. "Aren't mutts the best dogs? Friendly and unique." *And forgiving?* "And Pi is a mutt."

"I guess." Windy starts walking again. Levi and I follow.

"It'll be okay," he whispers to me.

I hope he's right.

27

The next day on the bus, Windy acts like normal Windy. Except her backpack is full of candy.

"I'm afraid if I left it at home, my mom would throw it in the trash," she says. "Do you want to count it?"

"No!"

"Relax." She elbows me. "I was joking."

I was up all night worrying that Windy would tell everyone that I was a genius. I imagined sitting in the cafeteria and Windy yelling, *Listen up, everyone. You need to know something about Lucy. This girl, my BFF, is a certified genius.*

But I also stayed awake worrying that she would be mad at me.

"Windy, I'm sorry I didn't tell you earlier."

"It's not a big deal," she says while sucking on a Toot-sie Pop.

"Well, it is to me. Can you not share—"

"You don't think I can keep a secret, do you?"

"No." I say it more as a reflex than a true belief.

"I won't say anything. I promise."

"Thanks." I open my backpack and give her my gummy worms. Her mom made her hand over all the sticky candy the moment we got home last night. ("You can't have that with braces.") I'm not trying to buy Windy's silence. Well, maybe I am, a little.

∞

In last period, I get an envelope addressed to *The Guardians of Lucille Fanny Callahan*. Everyone gets an envelope. They're 4 by 6 inches in size, white, and sealed. Still, some kids open them.

"Report cards?" I whisper to Windy.

"Yep." She tears hers open. "Yes!"

"Bring these back tomorrow, signed," Mrs. Shields, our social studies teacher, demands. "I'll give everyone who brings it back promptly 5 extra points on your next quiz." Mrs. Shields loves to give out bonus points. 3 points for having a sharpened pencil. 5 points for being in your seat on time when she has a sub. 10 points for bringing in interesting newspaper articles.

I hold on to the white envelope all through class and still have it in my hands when I get on the bus.

"Just open it," Windy says. "What are you afraid of? Is it because you're supposed to be a genius?"

"I am a genius," I whisper. Maybe she doesn't want it to be true.

I've been working hard to be an unimpressive A student. I try to get a few wrong on every test. I skip 1 out of every 9 homework assignments in each class to keep my grades in the very low A range. I never participate in class, but that's for other reasons.

Windy finally pulls the envelope out of my hands.

"Hey!" But I'm too late. She's already slid a finger under the flap and has it open. She hands me the folded sheet of paper.

"Do you want me to look 1st?" she offers.

"No!" I open the single page. I have A's in all the classes except math and language arts. Ms. Fleming gave me a B, and math doesn't even have a grade. It has an I for Incomplete.

"That's not awful," Windy says over my shoulder.

I look back at the report. Each class has a comment. And they are pretty much the same.

Lucy is a conscientious worker.

Lucy's work is of a high standard.

Lucy needs to participate more in class discussions.

Mr. Stoker's comment is the only truly original 1: *A parent-teacher conference requested.*

I fold the paper and put it back in the envelope.

"How did you get an Incomplete?" Windy asks.

"I don't know." I wonder how Levi did in math. He's on MathWhiz daily, and the few grades I've seen have been better. He had a 79 on the last quiz.

"My mom is always like, 'Do your best, Windy. That's all anyone can ask.' But I know if I got less than an A, she'd flip." She pushes her hair behind her ears. "Luckily, I got all A's. You know what that means?"

"Honor roll?"

"No...well, yeah. But that's not what I'm talking about. My mom promised me an epic birthday party if I got straight A's. I told you that."

"That water park place..."

"Rocky Mountain Lodge." She squeezes my arm. "It's going to be awesome."

"Sounds fun."

"Your nana isn't going to ground you for getting an Incomplete, is she? Because you have to go."

"I've never been grounded."

"Good. I'm inviting all the girls in our homeroom. Well, my mom is. She's worried I'm not trying hard enough to make friends. But it wouldn't be fun without you."

"All the girls? That's 13."

"I know. We'll have to get a suite. They have these cool rooms with sets of bunk beds. And each of them has a TV mounted over the bed."

"Do you think Maddie will go?" I've never seen Maddie outside of school, and I'd like to keep it that way.

"I'm sure. She's been to all of my birthday parties. Our moms are best friends."

"Yeah, you've mentioned that. And you and Maddie used to be superclose." My voice comes out mocking and mean.

Windy gives me a sideways look like I'm speaking in a different language.

"What about Levi?" I ask quickly.

"No boys. It's a sleepover." Windy doesn't stop talking about her birthday until she gets off the bus.

"I'll call you later, and we can talk more about it."

If Nana does ground me, that wouldn't be the worst thing. Then I could avoid the water park friend fest.

∞

No such luck. Nana laughs when she sees my report card.

"Is this your 1st B?"

"Yeah."

"Maybe we should hang it on the fridge." She smooths the paper and then admires it like a work of art. "And what's the I for?"

"Incomplete."

"Ahhh. Are you still pretending to be dumb?"

"Not dumb. Normal." I snatch the paper back. We are not displaying it anywhere.

"Well, it's dumb to pretend to be something you're not."

I stomp off to my room—ignoring Nana's pleas for me to come back—and log on to my computer. Here, I don't have to pretend. I join a calculus chat.

LightningGirl: anyone need me???

HipHypotenuse: always!

28

We go to the Pet Hut on Friday after school. I check out the dogs and plug their data into my formula—in my head.

"This is the winner." I point to a black Lab named Flint. (His estimated wait is 20 to 24 days.)

Windy pulls a leash and harness from the wall, and Levi opens the kennel.

"I'm going to see Pi." Taking pictures and getting to know the dogs is not my favorite part of our project.

I quietly knock on the office door before opening it. No one is inside. No one ever is.

"Hey, Pi." But my dog doesn't greet me like usual. I

walk around the desk and pull out the chair. No dog. Only my green-and-yellow sweatshirt.

I go to the front desk, where Noah is reading a textbook.

"Where's Pi?" I ask.

He shrugs. "With Claire. They were going to the vet's."

"Again?"

"I don't know."

I wait in the office. I enter 3 adoption forms into the computer. I fill Pi's water bowl. Levi and Windy finish taking pictures of Flint. They put up the new post, complete with a picture of Flint catching a Frisbee in midair.

"I like your action shot," I tell Levi.

When they finish, I stall and suggest they put up another post. "There's a Chihuahua mix in the 2nd kennel on top. I think his name is Marty."

While Levi and Windy are walking Marty, Claire finally returns with Pi.

"Oh, Lucy. Hi."

Pi runs across the office and leaps into my lap. I catch him like a football. He licks my face. He's the only animal on the planet that I'd allow this honor.

"I was getting worried."

I'm talking to Pi, but Claire answers for him.

"Lucy, we need to talk." She makes an exaggerated sad face and takes a seat on the corner of the desk. "There's no easy way to say this. You see ... Cutie Pi is sick. Very sick. He has cancer."

"No," I say. "That's not right."

"I was just at the vet."

I rub Pi behind his ears. He closes his eyes and stretches his neck. His tail wags, and his whole body vibrates.

"I'm sorry, Lucy."

The office door opens without a knock. Windy and Levi come in.

"I guess you found your dog," Levi says. "You were panicking for nothing."

I put my chin on top of Pi's head so I don't have to look at my friends.

"You okay?" Windy asks.

"I just told Lucy the awful news," Claire says. "Cutie Pi has cancer. He has a tumor at the base of his brain. You may have noticed that he tilts his head a lot."

I did. I thought he was inquisitive.

"The vet ran an MRI," Claire continues. "Which is like an advanced X-ray. Cutie Pi has a tumor the size of a Ping-Pong ball. It's affecting some motor skills and will gradually get worse. He may lose balance, walk into things, be unable to control his bladder."

Windy stands over me. She puts a hand on my shoulder and her other hand on Pi's back. "Poor dog."

"I'm glad y'all are here. I wanted to give you a chance

to say good-bye." Claire clasps her hands and pulls them to her chest, almost like she's praying.

"Good-bye?" Windy repeats. "He's not going to die right now."

Claire shakes her head. "No. Someone from animal control is supposed to pick him up today or tomorrow."

"You said if we did the data entry, you'd keep him." I want to pull out a signed document or show a video of our conversation. I need physical evidence to remind Claire that she promised to help Pi. But I have nothing to show her. My hands clench into empty fists.

"What's going to happen to him?" Windy asks.

"Don't make her say it. You know what's going to happen," Levi says.

"We cannot adopt out sick dogs. There are too many healthy animals that need homes. I'm sorry." Claire frowns.

"But you said you'd keep him if we volunteered for you. We've entered 239 adoption forms into the computer. That has to be worth 1 dog's life."

"That was before I knew his condition. I'm sorry." Claire crosses her arms and hugs her chest. She wants to rescue animals, but she has to think about the numbers, too.

"You can't do this. I'll adopt him. I'm taking him home with me. You aren't going to kill him."

"Calm down." Windy squeezes my arm.

"Lucy, let's go for a walk. Let's get some air," Claire suggests.

Pi looks up at me, his head angled. His mouth hangs open, which makes it look like he's smiling.

"Fine." I stand up and hold Pi in my arms. Claire probably expects me to put him on the ground. I refuse to let go.

She pulls open the door. I follow her to the trails in the back, where volunteers walk the dogs.

"I needed to get out of that office," Claire says. "Clear my head."

I nod. Pi wiggles in my arms. He's not trying to escape. He's trying to get comfortable.

"Lucy, I know you can't adopt Cutie Pi. I've seen you 2 together. If your family was able to take in a dog, he would have gone home with you weeks ago."

"I know, but . . ."

We walk down a muddy path. I stumble on a root, then catch myself.

"Here. Let me carry him," Claire says. "He must be getting heavy."

She right. He's heavy and squirmy. Pi's not happy about the handoff at 1st. I rub his head and tell him it's okay. But nothing is okay.

"I know we could find someone to adopt Pi. We will put him on our blog. I bet he has 30 phone calls on the 1st day."

"It's against our policy. Lucy, I'm sorry."

"It's not fair! What if someone *wants* to adopt him?"

"He's not available for adoption. We cannot ask a family to pay $175 for a terminal dog. There are too many—"

"Then just give him away," I say. "Free dog to a good home."

Claire stops walking and looks up at the cloudy sky.

"You have to give him a chance. Please." My eyes fill with tears. I want to wipe them away, but I can't. Touching your eyes, nose, or mouth is an easy way for bacteria and germs to get into the body. I try to use the sleeve of my jacket.

Pi looks from her to me. What good is it being a genius if you can't help 1 dog?

Claire's chin trembles. The rims of her eyes are red.

"Are you okay?" I ask.

She nods. "When I was a kid, I hated it when adults told me, 'Life's not fair.' I understood, but it always felt like giving up. And I was just about to say the same thing to you. Life isn't fair."

I take Pi back so she can wipe her tears.

"I'm sorry," I say.

"For what?"

"This isn't your fault. You want to help animals. I know that." She always smells like dogs and seems to work every day. She would help if she could.

"So do you and Levi and Windy." She smiles.

"No." I shake my head. "I don't care about the animals. I mean, I don't want bad stuff to happen to them, but I don't love them or anything. I'm more interested in the numbers. I didn't care about Rufus, Murphy, Flint, Jesse, or any of them." I hiccup. "But Pi. He's different. That's all."

"I didn't mean—"

"I hope you don't think I'm a bad person." My nose runs, and my eyes are scratchy. I take a deep breath. "I read that 670,000 dogs are killed in shelters each year. And I only care about 1 of them. I'd let all the other dogs go if I could save Pi."

"I don't think you're a bad person." She goes to hug me but stops. I've pulled away from her before. "I'll keep Cutie Pi here for a bit longer, okay?"

"Really?"

"Let's give it a try. You can put him on the blog. But he's not officially available for adoption."

I nod. "He's free to a good home."

"Make sure you're honest about his condition. It's a tough situation. We don't want to trick anyone into falling in love with a terminally ill dog. We have to be honest. Okay?"

"Okay. And thank you."

"Thank you, Lucy. I love all these dogs, but sometimes I forget what it's like to love just 1."

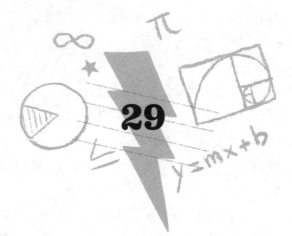

Pet Hut Dog Profile Blog

November 2—Meet Cutie Pi

Cutie Pi is a 6-year-old (approx.) beagle-husky mix with terminal brain cancer. He was abandoned at the Pet Hut shelter on September 18. He eats 2.5 cups of kibble per day. His life expectancy is less than 1 year. Cutie Pi likes kids (middle school–aged). He prefers a nonsmoking house and likes to be called Pi.

There's no adoption fee because this is not an adoption. Free to a good home.!!!!!!!!FREE!!!!!!!!!

I create the post for Pi. If I had money, I'd hire a marketing person or a journalist to do it. The lightning strike did nothing for my writing skills. Pi deserves better than my best. I make sure to be honest and use lots of exclamation points. Levi adds 8 pictures of Pi—double the number of photos we usually put up for a dog. In 2 of them, Pi wears my green-and-yellow sweatshirt. I know he's going to find a home. And for extra good luck, I ask Nana to pray for him.

30

Nana schedules the parent-teacher conference for Tuesday at 7:00 a.m.

Yesterday, I asked Mr. Stoker what he wanted to talk to her about. I knew I couldn't be failing math. I've got the numbers to prove it. He just said, "I want to talk about 1 of my favorite students." That wasn't a lot of help.

Nana follows me into the school and to room 213. The door stands open. Mr. Stoker sits at his desk working on papers. I stop and grab Nana's arm before we go in.

"Please don't tell him I'm a savant," I whisper. I'd like to think my favorite teacher wouldn't treat me differently if he knew, but I can't be sure. He might demand that I be switched to a different class, claiming it's for my own good. That's not a chance I'm willing to take.

She gives the smallest nod—and a giant eye roll—and then goes into the classroom.

Mr. Stoker gets up and greets Nana with a handshake. "Nice to meet you." Then he directs us to sit in the front row. No one pays attention to me as I clean the desk that Max Christie usually sits in or when I take 3 tries to sit.

Mr. Stoker perches on his stool.

"Let me start by saying that Lucy is a wonderful student. She may not always do her work, and she may not put in a full effort, but I can tell she is fascinated by my class."

I sink a little in my chair.

"She pays attention, and when she has the courage to ask questions, they're deep, thoughtful questions. More than once, she has stumped me. Sent me scrambling back to my college textbooks."

"But she's not doing her work?" Nana asks.

Mr. Stoker reaches over to his desk and grabs a grade book. "She's missed 4 homework assignments. I have a feeling that she completes the assignments but perhaps forgets them at home or on the bus."

I shrug.

"And what are her grades like? Is she failing?" Nana asks.

Mr. Stoker laughs. "No, no. She's scored between a 92 and a 95 percent on every quiz and every test."

He doesn't realize it takes me longer to get a question wrong than it does to get it right. I even show my work and make mistakes in either the method or the calculations. And I never do the bonus problems.

"That's pretty good," Nana says.

Mr. Stoker clears his throat. "I feel Lucy is holding back. I know she's new to public school. There are enormous pressures." He smiles at me. I turn away. "Perhaps you are afraid of doing well."

"I'm doing okay."

"Yes, you are," he says.

"Lucy," Nana says. "You're the only 1 who knows what's going on in your brain. Is there something you need to tell us?"

I shake my head.

Nana sighs.

"Lucy." Mr. Stoker looks at me. "I don't want you to be afraid to fail or succeed in my class. Does that make sense?"

I nod because I want to believe him. Then I look at Nana.

"She'll try harder," Nana says. "Now I have some questions for you."

"Certainly."

"Is she making friends? Is she fitting in?" Nana holds out her empty hands. "These are things that aren't on the report card."

"Nana, stop."

"We are considering sending Lucy to another school next year. It's a sort of boarding school, and I need to know if she can handle it. In your honest opinion."

"Well..." Mr. Stoker pauses, scratching his mustache. "We'd hate to see her go, but I'm sure she'll do well wherever she ends up. What do you think, Lucy?"

"I guess."

"So, she's making friends?" Nana asks again.

"Maybe Lucy can answer—"

"Yes, I have friends. Please, Nana, stop."

"Her group for the Cougars Care Project is doing some great work," Mr Stoker adds. "I'm impressed with their commitment to the project and each other."

I wonder if he heard about language arts class. Maybe Ms. Fleming cornered him in the teachers' lounge and told him about Windy and Levi's stance after I refused to read aloud. Does he know we were kicked out of class?

"Good." Nana stands up. "I'm proud of you, Lucy. But if you miss another homework assignment, you will lose your computer for a week. And no TV. Or candy." She gives me a hug.

"It was nice meeting you, Mrs. Callahan."

"Take care of my girl. She's 100 percent ordinary. Normal. Plain. Boring. Average." Nana winks at me, and I beg with my eyes for her to stop. "Absolutely nothing special about her."

Mr. Stoker laughs like he's in on the joke, and, for a second, I worry that he is.

"Good-bye," I say through gritted teeth. I love Nana, but sometimes I'd like a more normal, plain, boring grandmother.

As Nana walks out the door of room 213, Maddie walks in. They practically knock each other over.

"Oh, excuse me," Nana says. She steps aside and lets Maddie in.

"Sorry, ma'am."

Please don't call me the cleaning lady. Not in front of Nana.

"Have a great day, Lucy." Nana waves and leaves.

I let out a breath I didn't know I was holding. Maddie rolls her eyes and walks over to me. She never talks to me unless there's someone else around to hear her hilarious insults.

"Are you going to this?" She slaps down Windy's birthday invitation on the desk.

"Yeah."

"Don't take this the wrong way, but don't you think Windy would have a better time if you didn't go?"

I blink over and over. How can I *not* take that the wrong way? "Um, are you going?"

"Of course." She shakes her head like I've asked a stupid question. "I've been to every 1 of Windy's parties. Every single 1. I wasn't going to go if she had it someplace stupid again, though. Like at 1 of her mother's spas. That's where we went the last 2 years. But this place is actually cool."

I shrug.

She picks up her invitation and sighs. "At least we'll have someone to clean the bathroom."

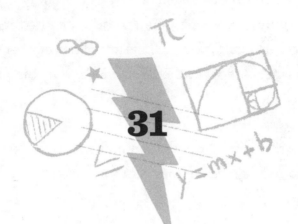

31

It's been 6 days since we posted about Pi, and he still hasn't found a home. Flint was adopted over the weekend, and even Marty, the yippy Chihuahua, had a few phone calls.

"What are we going to do?" I ask Levi at our lockers before homeroom. "Claire's not going to let him stay at the Pet Hut forever."

"I don't know. We can share his pictures again." We've already put Pi all over social media. Levi's moms have helped, and so have Ms. Sitton and Cherish. Nana wanted to help, too, but she couldn't remember her password.

"We need to do more."

"We need to go to class," Windy says, coming up be-hind me. "But I'll write up a new blog post later. Some-thing with more excitement. More adjectives."

We take our seats—me 3 times. We listen to morning announcements. Then Mr. Stoker starts math class.

"I'm not a fan of pop quizzes," he says. "But some-times they are a necessary evil." He goes to his desk and grabs a stack of papers.

Groans fill the room. I add a heavy sigh. I don't mind a math test, but I'd rather listen to Mr. Stoker talk and explain mathematics in his simple 7th-grade way.

"It would be faster if he just wrote F on the top of the paper," Levi says under his breath.

"I bet you get at least a C," I whisper.

"Gee, thanks."

"Think of it this way," Mr. Stoker continues. "It's more a test of my teaching skills than a test of your compe-tence." He hands out the papers facedown.

"Does that mean you get the grade?" Derek asks.

"Nope. Sorry. The grade is all yours. If I told you it wasn't for a grade, you wouldn't try your best. A grade is your motivation."

"Pizza's my only motivation," Derek says.

Mr. Stoker places a test on Levi's desk and then on mine. When all the papers have been handed out, he tells us to start and turns on some classical music.

I expect the test to be a review of perimeter, area, and

volume. And the 1st page is. But the 2nd page is a complex word problem. I glance at Levi's test.

"Eyes on your own paper," Mr. Stoker says, obviously watching me.

The problem in front of me is hard. Really hard.

The octagon P1 P2 P3 P4 P5 P6 P7 P8 is inscribed in a circle, with the vertices around the circumference in the given order. Given that the polygon P1 P3 P5 P7 is a square of area 5, and the polygon P2 P4 P6 P8 is a rectangle of area 4, find the maximum possible area of the octagon.

Immediately, I know that the diameter of the circle is $\sqrt{10}$. But that's all I can do in my head.

There's no way anyone else has the same test. This is not middle school math. Maybe not even high school. I try to work and rework the problem in my brain—never write anything down—until Mr. Stoker collects the papers. He spends the rest of the class going over the answers. He does perimeter, area, and volume. He doesn't mention the special problem on my page 2. I can't concentrate. My brain is stuck trying to find the area of the octagon.

I tap my toe 3 times under my desk. But I'm still focused on the problem.

When the bell rings, I'm slow to get up on purpose. I tell Windy I'll see her later, and I approach Mr. Stoker.

"You didn't give me the same test as everyone else," I say, staring at the floor.

"Every student is unique," he says. "Sometimes I create unique tests." He goes to his desk and picks up the pile of quizzes.

"That's not fair."

"It's certainly fair. It's not equal. That's the word you were looking for. *Equal.*" He pulls my paper out and turns to the 2nd page.

"You didn't teach us this."

He shrugs and points at 1 of his posters. "The Pythagorean theorem has been on the wall since the 1st day of school. You know how to calculate area. You know an octagon has 8 sides. You know the angles—"

"You didn't teach this!" I say again. But he's right, and that makes me angry. I know all the elements needed to solve this. Why can't I solve it?

"You didn't even try it." He taps the sheet.

"I can't do it."

"Maybe not." He actually smiles. "I haven't solved it myself yet. It's from an old Putnam Competition. That's the major collegiate mathematics contest."

He stares at me, waiting for a reaction. I don't move. I don't blink. I don't say anything.

"Well," he continues, "I'll let you know if I come up with the solution."

What kind of teacher gives out a problem he doesn't have the answer to? My cheeks feel hot, and I'm not sure whether it's from frustration or excitement.

Mr. Stoker tears the 2nd page off and gives it to me. "In case you want to work on it at home."

I shove the paper into a notebook and leave. The problem gnaws at my brain during Spanish. I scribble on an imaginary whiteboard in my head. I plug in the numbers. Their colors and shapes get messy, like I'm forcing them to play along when they don't want to. I erase the mess in my brain and restart again and again.

I can't take it anymore. I raise my hand and ask Señora Hubbell if I may use the bathroom. She says *sí* and doesn't question me when I take my notebook and pencil along.

As I run down the hall, I pull out a Clorox wipe. I use it to push open the door to the bathroom and again on the stall handle. Standing over the toilet, I write down the 1st half of the answer. The easy part. It takes me 9 minutes to work out the rest of the problem.

I got it! It actually wasn't *that* hard once I put pencil to paper.

I want to show Mr. Stoker that I figured it out. Maybe leave it on his desk. But I can't. I stare at my solution, lost in the beauty of it. The way an art lover would look at a painting in a museum. Then I tear it into little pieces and flush it down the toilet. Unlike an original artistic masterpiece, I can do the problem again, and it will be just as beautiful.

32

Windy's birthday is Saturday, and Pi still hasn't found a home. His blog has 17 comments—all different ways of saying *poor puppy*. I don't want to go to the party. I want to go back to the Pet Hut. But Nana knows about the sleepover—and how excited Windy is—and she won't let me skip.

Windy invited every girl in our homeroom class to her celebration at the water park, and 9 said yes, including Windy. Nana takes me to Target to buy a new bathing suit for the occasion. It isn't the right season for swimming, but we find a pretty 1-piece that is a size too big on a clearance rack. We buy it anyway. I can't find any water shoes on the shelves, so my old pair will have to do.

"We need to get Windy a gift," Nana says, admiring a tie-dye craft kit also in the clearance section.

"I'm making her gift."

"Oh. Great."

I hope so. Maybe only grandparents like homemade gifts.

With so many girls going, Ms. Sitton takes 5 in her SUV, and Maddie's mom drives the other 4. I can't believe I'll be spending 32 hours with Maddie.

I text Levi from the car.

Me: let me know if Pi gets adopted

Levi: don't get your hopes up

Hope is all I have.

Me: you should adopt him

Levi: I can't

Me: did you even ask your moms

Levi: 1000 times

Me: stop being inaccurate

Levi: I asked at least 5 times

Levi: I'll ask 1 more

Me: THANKS!

Levi: try not to drown

Levi: and try not to drown Maddie

∞

We get to the water park at 1:58. The place is bigger than an airport. While Ms. Sitton and Mrs. Thornton check us into the hotel room, all the girls use their cell phones to take selfies and post them on the Internet. Windy makes sure I get in a few of the pictures. I try to smile as big as everyone else as I tap my toe 3 times.

"When can we go on the rides?" Maddie asks.

Ms. Sitton hands out the bracelets that are our tickets.

"Let's drop our stuff in the room 1st. Then we can all change into swimsuits." Ms. Sitton is talking about me. All the other girls wore their swimsuits under their clothes. They need to strip off their T-shirts and pants, and they'll be ready to dive in. I wish someone had told me to layer up.

We shove into the elevator with our 17 bags. Even the elevator smells of chlorine and has a wet floor. Windy smiles at me and squeezes my hand. She's so happy; I feel guilty for dreading every minute of this.

The room—a suite—is huge. It's bigger than the apartment I live in. Someone has hung streamers and tied up balloons. I count 30 of them.

"Awesome," Daniela says, admiring a basket of snacks on the table.

"We're sleeping in here." Windy points to a room that looks like an old log cabin.

Everyone runs to pick a bed. I get there last, and Maddie has already taken the bunk with Windy. For someone who usually can't stand breathing the same air as Windy and me, Maddie suddenly can't get close enough to Windy.

"Are you okay with the cot?" Windy asks. A rollaway sits in the middle of the room.

"It's fine," I lie. I want 1 of the cool bunk beds. They look like canoes, and each has a TV mounted on a swivel arm. But it's not my birthday. This is all for Windy.

I don't carry my Clorox wipes down to the water park. I tell myself that the chlorine in the water will be enough to kill the germs.

We show the employee at the door our wristbands as we go inside.

"He's cute," Maddie whispers to Windy. "And he was checking you out."

"Really?"

The guy has to be at least 18. Still, Windy giggles and kind of dances as she walks. I pull my bathing suit straps tighter so I don't have such a big gap in the front. My lightning-bolt charm swings from my neck. I should have taken it off, but I'd feel even more naked without it.

"Girls!" Ms. Sitton has to yell to talk to us over the sound of rushing water. "We need to find a central spot, and then we'll go over rules."

Maddie's mom points to some free lounge chairs. We throw our towels and beach bags down. The other girls kick off their flip-flops. I keep my too-tight water shoes on.

"This place is so cool," Maddie says. She looks different when she's happy and not scowling at me.

"Madison," her mom says, "will you please stand up straight? And ..." She pats her own stomach.

Maddie stops smiling. She pulls her shoulders back and sucks in her stomach. Mrs. Thornton gives her a little nod before turning to help Ms. Sitton. Maddie doesn't move. I'm not even sure she's breathing. It's like all the excitement and happiness drained out of her in that moment of good posture. Then she catches me watching and gives me her death stare.

"What are you looking at?"

I don't answer. Instead, I focus on rebraiding my hair.

"We're going to use a buddy system," Ms. Sitton says. "No one goes off by themselves. Got it, girls?"

Immediately, everyone starts grabbing hands. This buddy-system business is serious. Windy gets pulled at from 2 directions—Maddie on her left and Daniela on her right.

"We're an odd number," Kaitlyn points out.

"We'll have 1 group of 3 girls," Ms. Sitton says.

"We'll be the truddy," Maddie says. She takes Daniela's other hand, and suddenly they are a circle-like shape. (But they don't have a true radius.)

This forces the other group of 3—Jennifer, Jasmine, and Kaitlyn—to break up.

"Jennifer, why don't you be a buddy with Lucy," Ms. Sitton suggests.

Jennifer puffs out a loud breath and takes a step

toward me. I put my hands behind my back, but she doesn't try to grab them anyway.

"We can switch partners in a few hours," Ms. Sitton adds.

"We can be buddies later," Windy says to me. "Okay?"

Then Ms. Sitton tells us her other rules: No leaving the water park area. The arcade and ice-cream shop are off-limits. We need to check in every 30 minutes at this spot. None of us have watches, and I don't see a clock, so I don't know how she expects us to keep time. I'm tempted to count seconds in my head.

"Stay with your buddy at all times. And have fun."

"What do you want—" I try to ask Jennifer.

"Come on," she says, following the truddy toward a staircase. It rises 4 stories high and is crowded with people.

"What is this ride?" I ask. They move too fast to answer me.

We climb 20 steps and join the back of the line. I manage not to touch anything, especially the metal handrail. I tap my toe 3 times.

We move slowly up the steps. More people crush in behind us. There's hardly room to breathe. Jennifer and the truddy form a small huddle, and I hang to the outside.

"This is the best ride," Maddie says. "I rode it like 1,000 times when I was here over the summer."

Not possible. Even with no line, I estimate it would take her at least 50 hours to ride it 1,000 times.

"I heard a 10-year-old died on this ride last week," Jennifer adds.

"It wasn't last week," Maddie says. "It was over a year ago. If it was last week, the ride wouldn't be open now."

My stomach flips. I'm not afraid of heights or going fast. I don't think anyone *actually* died on the ride. It's the used Band-Aid on the next step that makes me ill. This place is very unclean. It's disgusting.

"Are you okay?" Windy asks me.

I force myself to nod (and not throw up). I'm not going to ruin Windy's birthday.

"Good," she says. "I just want everyone to get along." Then she whispers to me, "Maddie is being so nice. I bet she's only doing it because her mom warned her or something."

I want to say, *And that's okay with you? She's being forced to be your friend for the day.* Instead, I shrug.

"We're almost there," Daniela says. We still have 2 flights to go, but we are close enough to read the warning sign. No pregnant women. No heart patients. You must be 48 inches tall to ride.

"4 people ride in 1 tube," Jennifer points out. "We can go together." She still has her back to me.

"But we're 5 people," Windy says. "Maddie, Daniela,

and I will go together, and you go with Lucy. She's your buddy."

"But if Lucy and I go together, then we are going to have to ride with them." With her thumb, she points to the father and son in line behind us. "I don't want to go with strangers."

As we travel up the next flight, they debate who should ride with whom. Windy's the only 1 who thinks 4 is the wrong answer. I don't say anything.

"I'll go with Lucy," Windy says, but Maddie makes a pouty face.

"It's your birthday. I want to go on the 1st ride with you. We used to ride carousels together. It's like tradition."

Windy bites her lip, like she can't decide.

"You don't care, do you, Lucy?" Maddie finally asks me. "I promise we'll wait for you at the bottom."

I shrug.

"Really?" Windy asks.

We are next in line.

"We'll take turns," Jennifer says. "Next time, someone else will ride alone." I don't think she's volunteering.

I watch as the 4 *friends* get into the clover leaf-shaped inner tube. Windy waves good-bye to me as the guy working the ride pushes them into a dark tunnel. The echo of their laughs and screams lasts long after they've disappeared.

"How many?" asks the guy, holding the next empty tube.

I hold up 1 finger. He points to a spot and asks the man behind me the same question.

I don't move. The father and son climb in, followed by a lady who's wearing long shorts and a T-shirt instead of a bathing suit.

"Come on," the employee says. "You're holding up the line."

"I'm not ready."

When the light on the wall changes to green, he sends the tube forward into the tunnel.

The next group is 4 teenage guys. They get in without hesitation. The light changes. The ride starts.

I watch another group of 4 and then 2 doubles, another set of doubles, another group of 4. When a group of 3 steps up—a mom and her 2 daughters, who are barely 48 inches tall—the worker gives me a choice.

"Get on this ride or go back down the stairs. You can't stand here. It's against the rules."

I take a step toward the stairs. I don't want to push past all the wet people, rubbing skin to wet skin.

"It'll be okay, sweetie," the woman says. "We went on it earlier."

"It's not that scary," says the girl with pigtails.

I step into the water and lower myself into 1 of the seats. I stand up. I sit. I stand up.

"Come on!" the guy yells.

I sit for the 3rd time, and the stupid jerk probably thinks it's because he yelled.

I don't want to hold the plastic handles. But when he pushes us into the dark tunnel, I grab on and close my eyes.

The ride is fast and kind of fun. I get water up my nose. And I scream louder than I ever have in my life. I imagine that the loops and twists are perfectly calculated equations. I'm riding math. As I step out at the bottom of the ride, I dunk my hands into the ankle-high water, hoping to clean off the germs.

"That wasn't so bad, was it?" the woman asks.

"It was kind of awesome," I admit.

She waves good-bye, and I look around for my buddy and the truddy group. They're gone.

33

I walk the outside loop of the water park, looking for the other girls. I bump into Jasmine and her buddy.

"Have you seen Jennifer or Windy?" I ask.

"Nope." They don't even stop.

I decide to go back to the chairs and catch up with them there.

"Hey, Lucy," Ms. Sitton says, looking up from her magazine. "Are you checking in?"

"I guess."

"Where's your buddy?"

"I don't know."

Her lips squeeze into a tight single line. She looks over at Maddie's mom.

"You were supposed to stay together," Mrs. Thornton says. "We explained that. Clearly."

"Sorry. It wasn't my fault. We got separated and—"

"Who was your buddy?" she asks.

"Jennifer."

Ms. Sitton sits up. "Her mother said she's not a very strong swimmer. I hope she's all right."

"Don't worry. I'll find her. You wait here in case she comes back." Mrs. Thornton stands and pulls on a cover-up.

"She's probably with Windy and Daniela and Maddie," I say, but Mrs. Thornton is already gone.

"This place makes me so nervous," Ms. Sitton says. I guess she's talking to me, since I'm the only 1 left. She looks out at the giant wave pool at the end of the room.

I wrap my towel around my waist and sit, stand, sit, stand, sit on the end of a chair. It feels like forever before Maddie's mom comes back with Jennifer and the truddy group.

"Where did you go?" Jennifer asks like I was her missing 2-year-old. "We couldn't find you anywhere."

"You never came down the ride," Windy says.

I don't bother to explain.

Ms. Sitton shakes her head. "I'm glad everyone is all right." Then she goes over all the rules again and insists that we sit down for 10 minutes and think about it. We are in middle school, and she's putting us in a time-out.

"Mom, you're embarrassing me," Windy says. Her cheeks are blotchy and red.

"I don't care."

I feel Jennifer's eyes trying to burn me. I want to tell her that she can't kill me by staring. Instead, I focus on my water shoes.

∞

We don't eat dinner until 8:30. Even with 3 bathrooms in our suite, it takes the group a long time to get ready. (97 minutes from the time we walk into the room—dripping and smelling like chlorine—until the time we walk back out in our nice clothes.) Everyone except Jennifer and me are wearing skirts or dresses. But Jennifer is still stylish in pants that look like purple leather and a shirt that hangs off 1 shoulder.

I wear a teal-and-pink-striped shirt (like the colors of 107 and 42) and dark jeans. I consider this my lucky shirt because it has a prime number of stripes: 17. It's harder than you'd think to find clothes with prime numbers in them.

After dinner, we go upstairs to the suite for Windy to open presents. I regret making my gift. *Who does that?* I should have bought the tie-dye kit.

Windy carefully unwraps my box. A smile spreads across her face as she reads the title of the book I made. *101 Other Things You Never Knew About Your Best Friend.* It's the sequel to the 1 we filled out at her house when I 1st spent the night. It took me 30 hours, 50 sheets of paper, 2 yards of ribbon for the binding, a pack of 12 markers, 100 stickers, and 1 ruler. And it wasn't easy. The original had the obvious questions, like what's your middle name, your favorite color, most embarrassing moment. My book asks what's your favorite prime number. If you discovered a planet, what would you name it? How many letters are in your whole name?

"That's cute," Maddie says when Windy holds it up. "We should totally fill it in."

Windy says thank you to everyone after opening each present. She doesn't seem to like any 1 gift more than the others, but it's obvious my present cost the least.

Maddie gives her a silver necklace that says *Windy* in scrolly letters. It's really cool and expensive. We all know it's really expensive because Maddie tells us. "The shipping alone was like $30 because we ordered it from New York. You can't buy jewelry with the name *Windy* off the shelf. It's got to be custom-ordered."

"It's awesome, Maddie." Windy gives her a hug.

After all the gifts are opened, I kind of wish Ms. Sitton would tell us it's bedtime. I also want her to say that there's been a change of plans and we need to leave 1st thing in the morning. She does neither.

"Have fun, girls." She turns on the gigantic television and tells Windy to order any movie she wants. "Just keep the noise down," she warns.

"And, Maddie." Mrs. Thornton leans over her daughter but talks loud enough for us all to hear. "Watch your diet. You have a gymnastics meet next weekend. You need to stay trim."

"I know, Mom." Maddie's cheeks redden. If Levi were here, I imagine he'd snap her picture at this moment. He could label the photo *rage* or *embarrassment* or *disappointment*. I'd tell him to send the picture to Mrs. Thornton because she doesn't seem to notice any of it.

Ms. Sitton and Mrs. Thornton go into their room and leave us alone.

I help Windy gather snacks from the little kitchen in the back of the suite: candy, cookies, popcorn, and chips, and not a single vegetable.

"Are you having fun?" Windy asks me.

I shrug but then force myself to nod.

"Me too." She smiles and does a little dance. "Best birthday ever! And everyone is being so cool. I was kinda worried."

"And don't you think that's weird?" I ask as I grab a pack of soda out of the mini-fridge.

"What do you mean?"

"Why is Maddie being nice to you? I mean, she's never—"

Windy interrupts me. "We used to be best friends. Are you jealous?"

"No, no." The only person I've ever been jealous of

is SquareHead314 when he/she finishes a problem faster than me.

"Good, because you're my BFF now. I've just known Maddie longer."

I nod and smile. Things will go back to normal next week. I hope.

"Where's the food?" someone yells from the living room.

"Coming!" Windy answers. I follow her back to the group. We pass out the snacks, and then I find a spot on the floor next to Jennifer's feet. My sit-stand routine—which everyone should be used to—is even more obvious when I'm trying to sit on the floor.

After watching 2 movies in the living room, I tell everyone I'm tired, which I am.

"I'm going to bed." I wish I were going to my real bed.

"Good night." Windy stands and gives me a hug. "I love your gift," she whispers.

I text Levi from my cot.

Me: I didn't drown

Levi: having fun?

Me: not really

Levi: it's almost over

Me: I'm stuck here another 14 hours

Levi: that's 50,400 seconds

Levi: I did that in my head

I laugh. I know he's using a calculator, but I appreciate his effort to make fun of me.

Me: good night

Levi: later, freak

I fall asleep pretty quickly. I think. Does anyone ever really know the exact moment they fall asleep? But when the rest of the girls come to bed later, they wake me up.

I turn over and keep my eyes closed. I guess I'm pretending to be asleep, though that sounds dishonest. I am *trying* to fall back asleep.

The girls laugh and joke around. They're pinching each other, jumping from bed to bed, and Daniela is trying to pull down everyone's pants. At least that's what I think is happening. My eyes are still closed.

"Shhh," Windy says, laughing. "Lucy is asleep."

"Yes, everyone, quiet," Maddie says, not quiet at all. "Don't wake her up. I can't deal with her anymore tonight."

Maddie does something that makes everyone laugh. Probably making fun of me.

"Let's hide her stash of cleaning wipes," Maddie suggests.

"Don't be mean," Windy says.

"Geez, I was kidding. I just don't get it." Maddie actually lowers her voice. "Lucy's okay for a little while. But I don't know how you hang out with her all the time."

I hold my breath, waiting for Windy to say something. I want to close my ears like I can close my eyes.

"She's cool," Windy says, rather unconvincingly. Like the way I'd say that all classes are as important as math.

"If you say so," Maddie replies.

"You really should give her a chance. She's nice, and she's funny. She's not good at painting nails, but she's smart. And she's helping a lot of dogs find loving homes."

"She also doesn't know how to be normal," Maddie says. A bed creaks again and again. Some of the girls laugh. "That kid who used to pull out his hair was more normal than Lucy. She's so—"

"Leave her alone. You shouldn't make fun of her. She was struck by lightning!" Windy blurts out.

My heart stops—if that's actually possible without a massive zap of electricity. The room is full of gasps. If I don't move, maybe I'll turn invisible. All I want is to disappear.

"What are you talking about?" Maddie's voice rises above the rest.

"Nothing."

"Windy, speak!" Maddie orders.

"Shhh," Windy says. "Lucy was struck by lightning in elementary school. It turned her into a math genius."

"Oh my god!" someone says.

Shut up. Shut up! I can't move. I'm too shocked. *Shut up. Shut up!*

"She's smarter than Einstein. She's smarter than Mr. Stoker," Windy continues. "She can do any math problem. How many geniuses do you know? She should be in college or working for some government agency. She's way smarter than any of us or anyone we've ever met."

I'd open my eyes if I thought I wouldn't cry.

"But what about the sitting and the cleaning?" Jennifer asks. "Is that because of lightning, too?"

"I guess," Windy answers.

"Whatever. Good at math and a human lightning rod—that's what you call cool?" Maddie asks. "Maybe she's smart. But she's incredibly weird. She's going to end up living alone in a basement with a bunch of cats. Windy, you used to have better taste in friends."

"Well ... it's not like you even talk to me at school. You've been ignoring me all year." I can't tell whether Windy's crying. "Lucy is the only one who wants to hang out with me."

"Windy, you're still 1 of my BFFs. We've known each other forever. We all love you."

"Yeah," Daniela agrees.

"Love you, Windy," another adds.

"Middle school is different," Maddie continues. "My mom says it's all about balance. I have to make time for my schoolwork, and my family, and gymnastics, and *all* my friends."

"You haven't found much time for me," Windy whispers.

"I will. I promise," Maddie says. "I was thinking. You should join my team for the Cougars Care Project."

"I already have a team," Windy says.

"You don't belong on that team," Maddie says. "You're not a weirdo. You don't need to hang out with the cleaning lady and that stalker kid with the camera."

Once she starts talking about Levi, I can't take it anymore. I sit up. The room gets quiet, and everyone looks at me.

"Sorry. Did we wake you?" Maddie asks with a voice full of knives. Everyone laughs. Everyone but Windy.

"Lucy, are you okay?" Windy asks. She takes a seat on the end of my cot.

"Leave me alone." I grab the pillow and walk out to the suite's living room.

"Lucy!" Windy calls. "Wait!"

"Let her go," Maddie says. "Don't let her ruin your birthday."

34

The next day, I sit in a plastic beach chair and count the words in a book while everyone else rides the waterslides again. We leave the park at 4:22, according to the clock in Ms. Sitton's SUV. I stare out the window for the entire drive. The other girls play a version of Would You Rather? I don't need to pretend to be asleep. No one even notices I'm here.

"She was a delight," Ms. Sitton says when she drops me off. "A very sweet and polite girl."

"Glad to hear it." Nana stands in the doorway. "What do you say, Lucy?"

"Thank you. I had fun." I was going to say thank you

before she prompted me, even though I hated almost every minute of the party.

I follow Nana into the living room. She sits down on the couch.

"I'm tired," I say.

"I bet. Did you have a good time?"

"It was all right."

I go to my bedroom and check the pet blog. Pi has 3 new likes and 1 new comment (*This is so sad. Hope Pi finds a forever home even if his forever won't be long*).

I text Levi.

Me: any news?

Levi: someone filled out adoption papers for Marty

That's good, I guess.

Me: Anything else?

Levi: no sorry

∞

We don't have school on Monday because of Veterans Day, and the Pet Hut is closed. So I spend my time looking for last-resort dog sanctuaries. There's a ranch in Tennessee called Sweet Dreams Farm that takes in sick and unadoptable animals. The dogs get to live there forever. But it costs $90 a month and is completely full.

On Tuesday, I still don't want to see Windy.

"I'm not going to school today," I announce as I walk into the kitchen.

Nana looks up from her bowl of cornflakes. "Are you sick?"

"No, I don't want to go." I grab a bowl from the cabinet.

"That's not how school works," Nana says. "You don't pick and choose when you go."

"I'm still tired." I shrug. "I didn't sleep at the hotel."

"What happened?"

"Nothing!" I snap. "I'm tired. And I'm not hungry anymore."

I throw my dish into the sink. It lands on a dirty glass, which shatters.

"Lucille!" Nana shouts.

I run to my room and close the door. The tears start before I can fall onto my bed. I don't do my sit-stand routine. I cry into my pillow and let the numbers flood my brain.

3.14159265358979323846264338327950288841 . . .

The numbers come in, and Windy stays out.

I wish I could make Nana stay out, too. This is her fault. I didn't want to go.

She knocks on the door. I don't answer. She lets herself in.

97169399375105820974944592307 . . .

She sits on my bed.

81640628620899862803 . . .

She pulls me into a hug.

4825342117067 …

I try to push away.

982148086 …

She hugs me tighter.

513 …

The numbers slowly fade.

Nana and I spend the rest of the morning on the couch watching the Travel Channel. We pretend that we are on a small tropical island that has no hotels, just little huts that stand in the water and come with butlers. Then we pretend to take the ultimate high-seas adventure on a cruise ship that has a carousel and an ice rink.

We order pizza for lunch. If this is what a sick day is like, I may never go back to East Hamlin Middle.

Windy texts me all day long from school, even though we aren't supposed to use our phones during classes.

Windy: Where r u

Windy: Why aren't you in school?

Windy: Are u sick?

I ignore them all. The 7th graders eat lunch from 11:10 to 11:35. I notice she doesn't send me any texts during this time, or right after. She must be too busy hanging out with Maddie. I'm only her friend when no one else will be.

Windy: will you be at school tomorrow

"Windy or Levi?" Nana asks when my phone buzzes again.

"Windy."

"She texts a lot. She must have quick thumbs."

"She does." I shove my phone under a couch cushion so Nana won't hear it and give me the do-you-want-to-talk-about-it look.

When a show about the best resorts for your dog comes on the Travel Channel, I suddenly don't want to be home anymore.

"Can you drive me to the Pet Hut?"

"Glad you're feeling better." Nana stretches. "Go grab my purse."

She drops me off and tells me she's going to get a Frappuccino and a *People* magazine, and that she'll be back in an hour.

Noah sits behind the counter. I'm starting to think he might live here. He looks up from the giant textbook he's reading. "Hey, your friend is outside somewhere."

There were no plans to meet today. For a second, I worry that it might be Windy, but she would have mentioned it in 1 of her 39 texts.

I use my sleeve to open the interior door. The dogs bark and growl, but it doesn't seem as loud as usual. Maybe I'm getting used to it.

I knock on the office door. No answer. So I let myself in, and Pi jumps on me. His paws leave dark smudges on my sweatshirt.

"You don't have very good manners." I rub his head. "But I'm happy to see you, too."

The stack of adoption papers on the desk is only 4 sheets tall. I quickly enter the data into the system. I like that the Pet Hut is now all caught up on paperwork. Pi lies in my lap as I work.

"Do you want to go for a walk?" I ask when I'm done. He knows the word *walk,* and he jumps from my lap and dances circles by the door. I slip on his harness and leash, and we go outside.

Levi is on the trail with an animal that looks more like a bear cub than a dog.

"What are you doing here?" he asks. "I thought you were sick."

Pi and the bear sniff each other—backsides, mostly. I guess middle school could be worse. This could be how we make new friends.

"I wasn't ... I'm not sick."

"Was it because of the stupid party?" He sticks a finger in his mouth like he's gagging.

I shrug.

"Because of Maddie?"

"I already knew she was a jerk. But now that Maddie and Windy are friends again, I might as well—"

"Wait. What? Maddie and Windy friends again? No way." His dog tries to pull him down the path.

"I swear it's true." Now I make the gagging motion. "They were *besties* all weekend."

"That friendship didn't last long," Levi says. "Windy

ate her lunch in the bathroom today after Maddie said something to her."

Gross. The bathroom. It's hard enough to eat in the bacteria-filled cafeteria. I almost feel sorry for Windy. Then I remember lying on that germ-infested cot, listening to the girls talk about me.

"So, what did Maddie say?" I ask. "Not that I care."

"Don't know. Don't want to know." He shakes his head, and then his shoulders drop. "And Windy wouldn't tell me. I did ask. She's annoying, but ya know, she's still a friend."

"Well, she's not my friend anymore." Saying those words hurts. I don't exactly have friends to spare. But if I can't trust her, what's the point?

"So, she told them all that you're Lightning Girl?" Levi gives me a sympathetic smile, and I can feel my neck get hot.

"What did you hear?"

"I heard that you're smarter than Einstein. That you've already graduated from college. And that you can move stuff with your mind." He wiggles his fingers in front of my eyes.

"Who said that?"

"Does it matter?" He shrugs.

"Ugh." I pull Pi closer to me. "I knew this would happen."

"What? That kids would talk about you for being

different? Wait like 5 minutes and they'll talk about someone else."

"This isn't going to go away. It's not like I wore the wrong brand of sneakers or dropped a tray of spaghetti in the cafeteria. I'm a freak. I scare people."

"Pi is scarier than you."

"You don't get it." I start walking back to the building. There's no use explaining.

"Lucy!"

"Leave me alone!"

"Whatever!" Levi yells after me. "You're the 1st person who has ever felt different. You're the 1st freak to ever set foot in East Hamlin Middle School. Congratulations, Lucy Callahan. You're so special!"

35

Nana gives me a ride to school the next morning because I *accidentally* miss the bus. I consider *accidentally* falling out of the car, but that would probably hurt. When I get to school, I practically run inside. I don't want to see Windy. I don't want to talk to her. I don't want to pretend that we are friends. Or that we were *ever* friends.

I throw my coat and my lunch in my locker and go right to room 213. The door's closed. I'm in such a hurry I open it without using a Clorox wipe. However, I do cover my hand with my sleeve. Once in my seat, I start working on the homework that's listed on the whiteboard. I keep my head down and let my hair hide my face. I wish the lightning strike had given me the superpower of invisibility. Sometimes, disappearing is the best solution.

"Lucy!" Windy shrieks when she walks in. "You're back." She makes it sound like I've been gone for weeks.

I don't look up from the math problems.

"You didn't text me back."

I shrug.

"You didn't have fun at my birthday party," she says. "Did you?"

Levi groans and slams down his books in the seat next to me. "God! If I have to hear any more about that stupid birthday party . . ."

"Don't be jealous."

"I'm not," he says. "Not at all. It's actually the number 1 thing I'm thankful for, that I did not have to live through your party."

Windy ignores him. "Lucy, do you want to come over after school?"

"No," I say.

The 1st bell rings, and Windy finally makes her way to her seat. She doesn't say hi to Maddie, and Maddie doesn't even look at Windy.

Mr. Stoker starts class with a review of the homework. He asks for someone to give the answer to the 2nd question, and Maddie raises her hand.

"I don't have the answer," she says. "I just want to say that Lucy Callahan should not be in this class. It's not fair to the rest of us. She has already taken this class. She's taken high school classes. Why is she here?"

"That's not appropriate," Mr. Stoker warns. "Keep those opinions to yourself."

Maddie makes pouty duck lips and rolls her eyes, basically sharing her opinion without talking. And for the 1st time, I realize that I don't care what she thinks.

"Well, I agree with Maddie," Jennifer says. "It's not fair." She smiles at Maddie, who nods.

"This is a class for 7th graders. You all belong here." Mr. Stoker speaks slowly in his deepest voice.

"I'm uncomfortable working in front of her," Maddie calls out.

"You'll have to get over that," Mr. Stoker says. He taps the marker against his palm.

"She messes up the class curve."

"I don't grade on a curve."

"She makes fun of me for not understanding this 'baby class' math," Maddie continues. "She makes fun of all of us."

I do not. I've never said anything.

"Leave her alone," Windy says. "She doesn't make fun of you."

"Excuse me! If anyone interrupts me again," Mr. Stoker snaps, "we will be having this conversation after school. Thank you." He turns back to the homework problem, and the class is finally quiet.

I ignore the lesson and Mr. Stoker. Maddie has successfully ruined my favorite class. Instead, I doodle in my notebook. I write the word *freak* and trace an outline around it over and over until I hit the edge of the paper. For someone who is supposed to be smart, I can't figure out how to get Pi adopted, and I can't figure out Windy. Why did she tell my secret to someone who is always mean to her? She chose Maddie over me. *Maddie.*

I put my arms across my desk and lay my head down. I'm useless.

Then I hear Maddie say my name with her usual disgust.

I look up.

"Enough, Madison," Mr. Stoker says. "I've warned you. You're staying after school to discuss this."

But Maddie keeps talking. "I find it very insulting when Lucy acts like this class is beneath her. She doesn't belong here."

"Shut up, Maddie," Levi says.

"Levi. None of that." Mr. Stoker points at him like he's accusing someone in court.

"Just stop," Windy says. "Please."

"I will not stop." Maddie sits up straighter. "She thinks she's better than us. I can't believe—"

"What do you want from me?" I shout. And the entire class freezes. Even Windy and Levi. Even Mr. Stoker. "I'm good at math. But what does that matter?" I point toward the whiteboard, at the problems that Mr. Stoker was in the middle of explaining. "Number 7, x equals 11. Number 8, x equals -1. Number 9, x equals 5." I give all the answers.

Mr. Stoker doesn't look surprised. "Lucy, you don't have to—"

"Yes, I do." I shove my chair back and get up. In 3 steps, I'm standing in front of Maddie. She shrinks into her chair. I've never scared anyone in my life. Not until now.

"What's your phone number?"

She tilts her head like Pi does. But it's not cute on her.

"What is your phone number?" I scream.

"555-993-9225."

"The sum is 54. The product is 5,467,500. The square root of 5,559,939,225 is 74,565."

I look around the room. Now Mr. Stoker *does* look surprised, like most of the class. Maybe even horrified. Only Levi smiles.

"I'm good at math. I'm great with numbers. But I don't know why this bothers you, Maddie. That is something I can't figure out."

She scowls.

"You try to put me down and make me feel bad. But there's nothing you can do that feels worse than having a sick dog and having a friend who . . . having someone you thought you could trust turn on you. Losing that person is what stinks." My nose starts running. I take a gulp of air like I'm drowning. "You don't matter to me."

Maddie stares at me. Her eyes fill with tears.

"You don't matter to me," I say again. Then I point to Levi. "He matters." Then Windy. "She matters. Or she used to. Until . . ."

Windy blinks hard, but I turn back to Maddie.

"You are nothing to me. You're just nothing. A big fat 0." I swallow hard and take a breath. "So stop trying so hard to ruin my life."

I need to get out of here. Away from Mr. Stoker and Windy and even Levi, who doesn't get it. Without taking any of my stuff, I run to the door. As it closes behind me, I think I hear someone call my name. I think it's Windy.

36

My heart crashes against my ribs. I can hear it in my ears and feel the thumping all the way to my feet. This should feel like a victory. I've confronted the enemy. It doesn't. I run down the hall and shove open the doors that lead to a small courtyard. The cool air fills my chest. I kick the stone bench that's engraved ELIZABETH MERRITT. JULY 19, 1993–FEBRUARY 12, 2005.

She lived 4,226 days. My stupid brain calculates Elizabeth's life without my ever giving permission.

What am I going to do?

I tap my foot 3 times. Maybe I'll get into NCASME. It was a mistake coming to this school. Nana's mistake. You don't need to be a genius to calculate that I don't belong here.

My breathing is almost back to normal when the door bangs open, and I jump.

"You can't be out here!" It's the assistant principal. "You should be in class."

"Sorry."

She steps closer.

"I didn't feel good," I say. "I needed air."

She holds open the door. "Let's talk in my office."

I spend the next 17 minutes answering questions and promising I will talk to a guidance counselor if I have any further issues. "I will." Then I'm finally allowed to call Nana. I tell her I have an awful stomachache and a headache and convince her to pick me up.

"Are you okay, Lucy?" Nana asks as we drive away from the school.

"Fine." I stare out the window and count.

"I thought you were sick." She glances at me.

"I am sick."

"Well then, what's wrong?" she asks.

"Nothing's wrong. I'm just sick. I need to go home." I wish Nana would stop talking.

"Okay. You can go home today. But we need to figure out what's making you sick, and soon, because tomorrow I've got my bowling league. If you call me during bowling,

I will not answer. I'm not missing it for anyone. Not even you." She tries to grab my hand, but I pull away.

"I said I'm not going back."

"The team captain is Mike Renwood. He's single and has hair." She keeps talking like I didn't say anything. "Well, some hair. Put it this way, for an over-60 gentleman, he's a 10 out of 10."

I know Nana is joking around. She wants me to groan or roll my eyes or say *gross*. But I'm not in the mood. She doesn't understand. I swear I'm not going back to that school.

When we get home, Nana demands that I sit at the kitchen table. I do my routine, and then she pops a thermometer in my mouth. While we wait for it to beep, she pours me a glass of orange juice, I'm not thirsty.

"The lady from the office said there was some yelling in math class. Do you want to talk about it?"

I shake my head.

The thermometer beeps 3 times when it's done. Nana pulls it out of my mouth.

"98.6. Perfectly normal. Lucy, what's going on?"

I'm not perfectly normal. I'm a freak. "Nothing is going on."

"Fine. Do you want to play a game?"

"No."

"Watch TV?"

"No."

"I need to run to the pharmacy. Do you want to come? We could stop for milk shakes."

"No."

"Suit yourself." Nana grabs her purse. "Get some rest. Tomorrow, you're going back."

The thought of sitting in Mr. Stoker's class again really does make my head pound. He's going to be disappointed or maybe embarrassed. And I never want to be in the same room as Windy again. Ever.

I watch from the window as Nana drives off to the pharmacy or wherever. The apartment walls feel like they're pushing in. I pace. 3 steps to the right. 3 to the left. 3 to the right. 3 to the left. The air stinks of kitchen trash. I'm gagging. I stomp to my room and slam the door. No one is around to hear it. My computer boots up, and I get on MathWhiz. Not many people are on in the middle of the day.

Numberlicious is debating some simple trig in complicated terms. He/she is an idiot. He/she doesn't deserve to be here.

LightningGirl: Numb, you don't know what you're doing!!!!!!!!!!

Numberlicious: Hey LG what's up

LightningGirl: Do you know anything at all? You're taking a stupid simple problem and making it complicated. You're a moron.

As fast as my fingers can move, I type up his/her mistakes and incorrect assumptions. And not only on this problem, but on every issue he/she has taken on in the past week.

My eyes are focused on the keyboard. When the computer beeps in protest, I look up and see a warning.

Numberlicious has blocked you from the conversation

"Fine!" I spend the rest of the day telling others—everyone—what they're doing wrong. I get blocked 3 more times.

Nana comes home, but she leaves again. Something about going to the library or bank or post office. I don't bother to listen.

My cell phone buzzes in my pocket. There's no one I want to talk to, but I look at the screen anyway. It's Uncle Paul. I know Nana must have told him to call me. *You talk to her. She won't listen to me.*

Why does Nana get to leave? I want to leave. I hate this apartment, and I hate East Hamlin Middle.

With nothing stopping me, I stomp out the front door. It closes behind me, and the lock clicks. I don't have keys or Clorox wipes, only my phone. Without thinking, I walk down the steps, through the parking lot, and past the bus stop at the end of the street. I turn right and jog across the 4 lanes of Route 68. Cars blare their horns. I hate them, too.

This area of town isn't meant for pedestrians. I tread through knee-high weeds, stepping over bottles and other garbage, heading to the Pet Hut. Not that I planned this. There's no way to accurately calculate how long it will take me. I don't know the exact distance or my walking speed. It doesn't matter. I have nowhere else to be.

The strip mall I pass is vacant except for a pawnshop. A guy stands outside smoking. He waves with his free hand. I want to run. Instead, I recite the digits of pi to keep myself calm.

3.14159 . . .

It works. I walk faster, stumbling over trash and broken pieces of pavement.

But then I come across the remains of a cat. It looks like it's sleeping except for the dried brown stain beneath it. The blood is the color of the number 55.

I can't step over the poor cat. I'm frozen on the side of the highway.

3.1415926535 . . .

The world fades until a big rig whips by me. The wind trailing it makes me stumble backward.

I pull out my phone. I call Levi.

"I'm scared," I say as soon as he answers.

"Lucy? What's wrong? Where are you?"

I tap my toe 3 times. "I'm going to the Pet Hut."

"Where are you?" he asks again.

"On Route 68. I'm walking to the shelter." I try not to sound terrified. My voice still shakes.

"What? That's stupid. Where's your grandmother?"

"I don't know."

"I'm going to call Windy and see if Cherish can pick you up."

"No. Not Windy."

"Lucy." Levi starts to say something, but I'm not listening. A navy-blue car has stopped next to me. My stomach tightens. I don't recognize the car and can't see the driver.

"Someone's pulled over," I mumble into the phone.

"Who?"

"I don't know."

"Don't get in the car with anyone," Levi warns.

"I know that!" I move away from the road, toward the chain link fence that surrounds a vacant lot.

"Are you okay?" a woman calls out her window. "Do you need a lift?"

I look back. "No."

The woman wears sunglasses and a smile. She isn't creepy in any way, but I still want her to leave. *Just go.*

"Lucy, what's going on?" Levi calls out.

The woman puts her window up and pulls away. I squat in the tall grass, hoping no other drivers notice me.

"Lucy!"

"I'm fine." My body feels full of energy that makes me want to fly. "Stay on the phone."

"Okay."

I make a wide circle around the dead cat. It's easier to breathe the farther I get away from it.

"Where are you exactly?" Levi asks.

"In front of a place called True Natural Turf." The brick building looks like a prison, with its chain link fence and barred windows.

"Okay. I'm pulling up a map online."

I walk quickly through the parking lot. My heartbeat echoes in my ears.

"You're over 2 miles from the Pet Hut, Lucy. The map says it'll take you 42 minutes to walk there."

"I can do it." In the distance, I see a sidewalk. Maybe the worst is over. "Stay on the phone." I say it again.

"I'm not going anywhere."

I believe him.

"Hey, I know what will make you feel better."

"What?"

"Math problems. Hang on a sec." I hear clicking in the background. "I got 1. Ready? Jane is counting her change. She has 2 more quarters than nickels, 5 fewer dimes than quarters, and 2 more pennies than nickels. The total amount is $1.86. How many coins does she have?"

"17."

"Geez, you answered it before I could even scroll down." He laughs. "Of course, you're right."

"I know."

"Do you want another problem?" he asks.

"Yes."

Levi asks me question after question as I walk. They're mostly simple algebra or geometry, but they still distract me from the traffic and from thinking about Windy. I answer 27 problems before I make it to the door of the Pet Hut.

"Don't walk home alone," he says.

"I won't. I promise."

"Text me later."

"Okay. Thanks for …"

"Yeah. No problem." He hangs up.

Math has saved me again. Or maybe it was Levi.

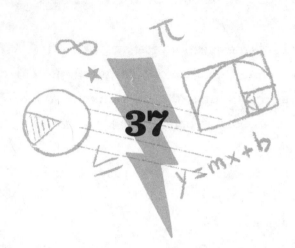

37

Noah waves to me from the front desk. A phone is tucked between his ear and shoulder.

This visit isn't planned, but I know exactly why I'm here. I need to see Pi.

All the kennels are full of barking, snarling dogs. Pi isn't in 1. He's the broken merchandise that's kept hidden in the back until it's time to throw it away.

I open the door to the office. I don't even get a chance to worry that Pi might not be there. My dog runs right to me. His body wiggles with excitement.

"Hi, Pi." When I kneel down in front of him, he jumps up and puts his paws on my shoulders. His tongue swipes my cheek, which is disgusting.

"Why are you so happy?" I ask him. "Don't you know I've had a rotten day?" It's like he does know. He nudges his nose under my chin over and over, trying to lift my head.

"Let's go for a walk." I grab his leash and harness. Pi jumps and runs in circles, making it hard for me to get him clipped in. I finally get it. He takes the other end of the leash in his mouth. I laugh.

"You're going to walk yourself? I don't think so." I wrestle my end free. We step out of the office and nearly knock into Noah.

"Sorry."

"No worries." He kneels in front of Pi and rubs his head. "I'm glad you came to say good-bye. Claire's been freaking out all day whether she should call you guys or just let it be."

"What do you mean?" I step back and pull the leash to my chest. "Is someone taking him? Has he found a home?"

Noah's face changes. I know Pi isn't being adopted—or given free to a good home. His time must be up.

"He's being picked up in the morning by animal control."

"No," I whisper. My throat tightens.

"Sorry." Noah reaches to touch my arm, but I pull away. "He's a good dog. You tried." He walks back toward the front desk.

Pi tugs on the leash. It's clear he really doesn't under-stand English. We were talking about his death sentence, and his tail is still wagging.

In the distance, I hear Claire talking to Noah. This is my chance. I should run away with Pi. I walked here. I can walk home. I can save him. But even taking 1 step feels like too many. I turn and go back into the office. Pi isn't happy to be shut inside. He scratches at the door.

"Stop it," I snap at him. "There's nothing for you out there. Nothing for either of us."

But Pi keeps pacing and digging to get out.

"Please. Stop."

He whines.

"Stop!" And he does for a second. I notice the black spot on his back. When I met him, I thought it looked like a lightning bolt. I thought it was a sign. But it really looks more like a *Z*.

My phone vibrates, but I ignore it, slamming it down on the desk. Pi stares at me with his head tilted. It's not cute and curious; it's the cancer.

I'm suddenly very tired. I can't even find the energy to cry or to care about bacteria and germs. I kneel down and crawl under the desk. My green-and-yellow sweatshirt is balled in the corner. I curl my knees to my chest and lay my head down on top. Pi wiggles his way in. He rests his chin on my shoulder. He's quiet and still, maybe for the 1st time ever. But somehow I know he's doing it for me.

He wants me to feel better and not be sad. He should be selfish and trying to escape, not cuddling up to me.

I wrap an arm around him. We both close our eyes. The digits of pi swim through my brain. At 1st, they're bright. Then they dim. My world is quiet except for the deep breathing of a dog.

$$\infty$$

A tap on the shoulder wakes me. I jump and hit my head on the bottom of the desk. Pi's rapid-fire tail bangs against my feet.

"Did you have a good nap?" Nana asks.

"No."

She offers me her hand and helps me out from under the desk. My knees and elbows and back ache. I glance at the clock on the wall. It's only 5:10. I slept less than 30 minutes.

Claire stands behind Nana. She forces a smile. I tap my toe 3 times and use globs of hand sanitizer.

"This must be Pi," Nana says. He sniffs and licks her sneakers. They probably smell like Cracker Barrel. She doesn't reach out to touch him. Nana doesn't like animals. She's 66 and has never had a pet in her life.

"Yeah, this is Pi. Can we keep him, please?" I ask, knowing I sound like a whiny little kid.

"Lucy," Nana says, which means no.

"They're going to kill him."

Claire sighs and closes her eyes. I wait for her to

correct me. She doesn't. She's probably thinking, *I'll never let kids volunteer here again. Too much trouble.*

"Let's go home, Lucy. It's been a long day." Nana gently takes my elbow. I pull my arm away like she's hurting me.

"I can't leave him!" I shout.

"Do you want me to take the dog outside?" Claire asks Nana.

"His name is Pi!" I snap.

"I know, Lucy." Claire keeps her voice calm and soft. "I love him, too. I know you don't believe that. But I do."

I want to be mad at Claire. I want to hate her. I can't.

"He's all I have." The words come out with the tears, and I'm ashamed right away.

"Am I chopped liver?" Nana tries to joke.

That makes me cry harder. Nana and Uncle Paul and math were once enough. I want to go back 79 days, before I cared about Pi and Levi. And definitely before Windy.

Nana turns to face Claire. "Pi is going to animal control tomorrow?"

"Yes, I'm sorry," Claire says.

"Can we keep him overnight?" Nana asks. "And I'll bring him to animal control 1st thing in the morning. I'd like to give Lucy time to say good-bye."

"If you think that's a good idea," Claire says.

"Honestly, I don't know. It's probably not. Maybe I should just rip off the Band-Aid now."

"No," I say. "Let's take him home. It is a good idea." It gives me 1 more night to find him a real home. And maybe Nana will change her mind. She might fall in love and want to keep him. We'd have to move apartments to some place that allows pets. It's all unlikely, but not impossible.

"It's only 1 night," Nana says, as if reading my mind.

"I know." Sometimes 1 is the perfect number.

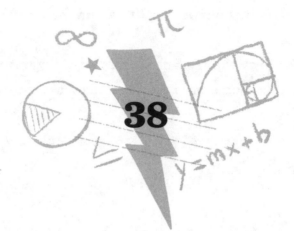

I leave the Pet Hut with Pi in my arms, knowing he'll never see this place again. I shuffle my feet so that my journey from the door to the car is exactly 29 steps. I need the luck of a prime number. I slip into the back seat.

Pi runs from window to window, almost happy. He doesn't get it. He lives in the moment. Like all dogs do.

Nana gets in the car. She turns the key, and the engine purrs. It's the only sound. She doesn't speak until we get on the road.

"How did you get to the shelter?"

"I walked."

Nana takes a deep breath. "For a smart girl, sometimes you make dumb choices."

"Sorry."

"I think it's time you tell me what's going on," Nana says. "I might not have a solution for you—especially if it has to do with math. But you'll feel better if you share your problems. I promise."

"This miscalculation has nothing to do with math."

We stop on a dead-end road for Pi to do his business, and I tell Nana about the birthday party and about math class. She listens quietly. She doesn't even joke.

I watch Pi gnaw on a stick. "I don't want to go back to East Hamlin. Ever."

"I get that," she says.

"I could go to the academy." I squeeze the leash tighter in my hand.

"Maybe. But that's not until January." It seems forever away. Anything beyond tomorrow feels like the next decade. I'm being selfish. I should be thinking about Pi. Only Pi. Not stupid Windy.

"I don't get why Windy would tell everyone."

"She screwed up."

"Don't defend her." I pick up Pi and carry him back to the car. I don't want to hear Nana take Windy's side.

Nana gets in and starts the car. She doesn't say anything else about Windy, but I'm ready with comebacks if she does.

Windy knew what she was doing.

Windy can't be trusted.

Windy never really was my friend.

Windy's a jerk.

When we pull into the parking lot, Nana throws me an old blanket she keeps in the car for emergencies.

"We will have to sneak him in," she says. "Wrap him up. And he'd better not bark."

"He won't. I promise." I stare at Pi, begging him to agree with Nana's rules. I carry the wriggling blanket to the front door of our building. I'm trying so hard to act normal that I don't notice Windy until she's a few feet away.

"Hi," she says, sitting on the steps. Her eyes are puffy, and she's pulled the hood of her sweatshirt over her head like she's hiding.

I walk past her and don't say anything.

Nana unlocks the door, and I go inside 1st.

"Come on in, Windy," Nana says, not considering what I want.

I tap my toe 3 times before letting Pi jump free from the blanket and onto our living room floor. His nose goes to the ground as he sniffs his new (temporary) home.

"Are you adopting him?" Windy asks, sounding hopeful. She helps herself to hand sanitizer.

"No. He's here only for the night," Nana says.

"Where's he going tomorrow?"

"That's my problem!" I snap. "Why are you here?" She was definitely not invited.

Nana gives me a hard look but then leaves the room. She makes an excuse about needing a shower and warns me again to keep the dog quiet.

"I don't want you to be mad at me," Windy says. She plays with the charm bracelet on her left wrist.

"Fine, I'm not mad at you," I lie. Windy looks up at me. She knows I'm lying, too.

"Yeah, you are. And I'm sorry." She says the last part really fast.

"Okay."

"You know what you said in math class?" Windy asks. "How I used to matter."

"Yeah?"

"I mattered to you, and I messed that up. And I don't know why I did what I did." She squeezes her eyes closed and takes a breath. "You have to believe me that I didn't mean to hurt you and tell your secret. I wasn't thinking. Maybe it was all the candy. A sugar overload."

Her stupid excuse makes my neck burn.

"I'm so, so sorry," Windy continues. "I'll make it up to you some way."

"You can't." I should say it'll be okay. But nothing feels okay. I never want to go back to middle school. And that's her fault.

"There must be something."

"There's not. You can't make this better." I walk out of the living room and into the kitchen. I fill a bowl with water for Pi, then wash my hands, scrubbing from my elbows to my fingertips in the hottest water.

Pi spills more than he drinks.

Windy leans against the doorway. Her arms are folded across her chest. "Can you please yell at me? Yell and scream and maybe throw something. But something soft. And then we can make up. Okay?"

"I don't want to."

"Yes, you do." She steps in front of me and grabs my shoulders. "Just do it."

"No." I knock her hands away.

"Then, do you forgive me?" she asks.

"Fine. I forgive you."

"So, we're friends again?"

"No."

She takes a step closer. "But if you—"

"You promised! You were my best friend, and you promised not to tell anyone. You just couldn't shut up for once."

Windy jerks back, and her mouth falls open. Pi scrambles between us.

"You tried to get the other girls to like you by making fun of me. Like I'm a joke. Look at the freak."

"I wasn't making fun of you. Is that what you think?"

"I was there! I know what you said." I clench my fists,

and my nails bite into my skin. "It doesn't matter why. You broke a promise. Don't you get that?"

I stomp across the kitchen. I open a cabinet and slam it closed. Then I open another.

"Lucy, it does matter why." Her voice is soft.

"Whatever." I pull out a bag of Twizzlers. I don't give any to Pi or Windy. Even though both of them look at me with sad puppy eyes.

"You're my best friend. I wanted them to like you, but all they ever get to see is your weird habits. The sitting over and over. The cleaning. I think your math tricks are totally cool. If I was a genius, I'd want everyone to know."

"So, you broke a promise because—"

"Geez! I know I broke a promise. And I said I'm sorry. So sorry." Her shoulders fall like she's exhausted, and she takes a seat on a kitchen chair. "I wanted them to be my friends *and* your friends."

For a second, I almost believe her. But then I remember lying on that cot and hearing all the girls laugh. "Why are we friends?"

She looks up. "What?"

"I don't understand. You've been nice to me since day 1 on the bus. Which makes no sense at all. Especially when I kept a secret from you for weeks." It was 65 days, to be exact. "Why would you want to be friends with me?"

She shrugs. "I don't know. Because you're a good person?" She says it like a question, and I groan.

"What's wrong with being a good person?" she asks. "You never complain about my love of musicals or my causes. You don't try to change people. It's like you're only trying to understand people."

I roll my eyes. I will never understand people. In algebra, you can solve an equation when you have 1 unknown variable. People are equations with dozens of variables. Basically unsolvable.

"You're different, Lucy," Windy continues.

"Yeah, I'm a freak genius," I mumble.

"That's not what I mean. Other kids care about clothes or what YouTube channels I watch. You only care that I use hand sanitizer. A lot of hand sanitizer. I think I may be developing a rash from overuse."

I almost laugh but stop myself by biting into a Twizzler.

"I guess you accept me for being me." She throws her head back. "Ugh, I sound like a guidance counselor."

"You really do."

"So as a guidance counselor, I have to ask, is there really no way for us to be friends again?" She bites her bottom lip.

I take a seat at the kitchen table (3 times, of course), and I hand her a Twizzler.

A smile spreads across her face. I wait for her to say something, but for the 1st time Windy Sitton is quiet.

I give her another Twizzler even though she hasn't

eaten the 1st, and Pi puts a paw on my thigh. He wants 1, too. I know dogs shouldn't have candy, but this is like his last meal.

"Tomorrow, he's going to animal control," I explain. "Tomorrow, he's going to be . . ."

"No. We can't let that happen. We're going to fix this."

"How?"

She pulls out her phone. "I might not have a lot of good friends, but I have a lot of contacts." She starts dialing. Levi's is the 1st number she calls. He's knocking on the front door 30 minutes later.

"Looks like we're having a party," Nana says when she lets him in. "I'll make popcorn."

Levi greets Pi with a tummy rub and some embarrassing kissy noises.

"Um." I clear my throat, and Levi looks up. "Thanks for helping me out earlier." I want to say more, like, no one else would have done that for me.

"Whatever. It wasn't a big deal."

"And maybe you're right."

He wrinkles his forehead. "About what?"

"Yesterday. You said I wasn't the 1st freak to feel out of place at school."

"Oh yeah." He stands up.

I play with my lightning-bolt necklace. "Do you really think this will blow over in 5 minutes?"

"Maybe. But now people will probably call you

Lightning Girl instead of the cleaning lady. Which is actually cooler. Isn't it?"

"Definitely."

Pi, not happy about the lack of attention, jumps up on me. Pi's right. Now is not the time to worry about my own drama.

"Can you update the blog post?" I ask Levi.

"I hate writing." He pauses. "But sure."

Windy keeps calling every number stored in her iPhone. Nana joins in, too, contacting her bowling-league pals and her coworkers. I try Uncle Paul.

"I've got the perfect dog for you," I say when he answers the phone.

"What?"

"I have a dog for you to adopt. He's cute and smart and—"

"Luce, I can't have a dog."

I knew it was a long shot. "Do you know anyone who does want a dog?"

"All my friends live in barracks. Not ideal for a pet."

Levi reposts to the website with a new heading. THIS DOG IS ON DEATH ROW. I stare at the computer, waiting for a miracle.

Every minute that ticks off the clock feels like a belt tightening around my gut. No one wants to adopt Pi. A friend of Nana's offers to call her daughter in Virginia to see if she's ready for a pet. She'd just moved into a big house over the summer. But that lead goes nowhere. It's after 10 when Nana drives Levi and Windy home. They each say a final good-bye to Pi before leaving, but I can't watch. I pretend to be busy in the kitchen.

"I'll ask my mom to repost Pi's picture and information," Levi says as he stands in the front doorway. "We'll find him a home."

"Thanks." I don't get my hopes up. Levi's mom has posted about Pi before.

I stay home with Pi while Nana drops them off. We go to my bedroom. Pi waits for me to sit, stand, sit, stand, sit before jumping into my lap. I click through websites, hoping to find a last-minute solution.

"Maybe I should let you go," I tell Pi. "You could survive in the wild. Eating out of trash cans and wandering the streets." Then I think of the cat on the side of the highway.

Like always, I end up on MathWhiz. I send a quick apology to Numberlicious, but he/she still has me blocked. So I go into a forum for math homework help. I answer question after question, from elementary school math to calculus. Pi rests his head on my right forearm, making it hard to move the mouse.

I keep working, even after Nana's home. Usually, solving the problems listed as *difficult* makes me feel better. Tonight, it's no help.

Suddenly, a chat pops up on my screen.

SquareHead314: you're working late

LightningGirl: bad day

SquareHead314: sorry

LightningGirl: not all problems are solvable

SquareHead314: True.

SquareHead314: Sometimes solutions take time

LightningGirl: I'm out of time

SquareHead314: Sometimes solutions take a team

I have a team. I have a great team.

SquareHead314: Let me know if I can help. You never ask for help.

LightningGirl: thx

SquareHead314: good night

I've been coming to the website for over 4 years, almost daily. And I've never once asked for help. There are some smart people here, but I'm a genius. Geniuses don't ask normal people for help.

I rub Pi's back. "I'm sorry," I whisper. He tilts his head.

"There's nothing I can do." This site isn't for selling old furniture or finding a plumber. I'd probably be banned for life if I wrote about Pi. I remember 1 guy last year asked people to sign a petition about coal ash being dumped in rivers. The guy was booted within an hour. My math friends can't help me.

Pi stretches and then puts his head down. He doesn't look comfortable, awkwardly sprawled across my lap and chair. But he does look happy.

"Fine! I'll ask for help."

I click on the logic-problem forum and start typing in all caps.

HELP! I HAVE AN UNSOLVABLE PROBLEM.

---

57 DAYS AGO I MET A DOG NAMED PI. (YES, PI AS IN 3.14159) I DON'T LIKE DOGS OR PUPPIES, BUT THIS FLUFFY BEAGLE MIX IS DIFFERENT. SPECIAL! AND NOT JUST BECAUSE OF HIS COOL NAME. HE KNOWS HOW TO MAKE A PERSON FEEL NEEDED. HE DOESN'T CARE IF YOU'RE SMART OR POPULAR. HE HAS NO CONCERN FOR PERSONAL SPACE. MAYBE MOST DOGS ARE THIS WAY.

TOMORROW HE WILL BE TURNED OVER TO THE HAMLIN COUNTY ANIMAL CONTROL. HE HAS CANCER AND IS CONSIDERED UNADOPTABLE. YOU CAN GUESS HIS FATE.

MATHEMATICALLY SPEAKING, IT DOESN'T MAKE SENSE TO ADOPT THIS DOG. HIS LIFE EXPECTANCY IS LESS THAN A YEAR (EXACT NUMBER OF DAYS UNKNOWN). HIS MEDICAL BILLS WILL BE HIGH (CURRENTLY INCALCULABLE, BUT PROBABLY HUNDREDS OF DOLLARS). BUT IF YOU CARE FOR HIM, PET HIM, HUG HIM, AND LET HIM LIE IN YOUR LAP, PI WILL LOVE YOU BACK (AND THAT CAN'T BE MEASURED, EITHER).

SOMETIMES NUMBERS AREN'T ALL THAT MATTERS.

PLEASE HELP SOLVE THIS UNSOLVABLE PROBLEM. IF

YOU CAN ADOPT PI, PLEASE CALL ANIMAL CONTROL AT 8:00 A.M.

IF NOT, LET OTHERS KNOW. PLEASE. PLEASE. PLEASE HELP.

HELP FIND PI A HOME, AND I'LL DO YOUR MATH HOMEWORK FOR THE REST OF YOUR LIFE.

I give the number for animal control, and I change my profile picture from a Fibonacci spiral to a selfie of me and Pi. A reply dings a second later.

JJillM: You can't post that here.

LightningGirl: Sorry it's an emergency

JJillM: There are rules. We can't put our personal problems up.

Numberlicious: Leave her alone.

2plus2: Where's Hamlin?

LightningGirl: North Carolina

2plus2: Crap. I'm in Canada.

MathMaster: :(

The next few hours go like this. Some people complain I'm abusing the system. Some say they live too far away. Some offer to send me money. None of these are solutions. At 2:30 a.m., I'm too tired to type anymore. I crawl into my bed in my clothes. Pi follows me.

"Do not lie on my pillow," I warn. We curl up together and don't move until Nana nudges me awake in the morning.

39

Nana sits on the edge of my bed, rubbing my back. For a split second, I forget that I'm sharing my sleeping space with a dog. I'm reminded by a wet nose on my cheek.

"Time to get up," she says.

"Have you changed your mind about keeping Pi?" I ask.

"I'm sorry." She stands and walks to the doorway. "Get ready. We need to leave in 15 minutes."

As soon as Nana closes the door, I check the math website and the Pet Hut blog. With each click, my hope slips away. It hurts to hold my head up, and my stomach is tight. So, this is what it feels like to fail.

I use the bathroom. Pi follows me. I get dressed. Pi stands at my feet. I have a frozen waffle. Pi gets 1, too.

"Hurry up. He probably needs to do his business," Nana says. She hands me my lunch. With all my school stuff packed up, I grab Pi and try to hide him under my coat. We rush to the car. No one notices.

Nana drives to the same dead end Pi used as a bathroom yesterday.

"Take your time," I tell Pi. "Take all the time in the world."

I wait for Pi to do number 1 and number 2.

"You gotta pick that up," Nana yells from the car. She holds out a plastic Walmart bag.

"I can't."

"You have to. It's the law." She rolls the window up.

I'm tempted to yell back, "He's not my dog!" But that seems cruel—especially in front of Pi.

While holding my breath, I pick up the warm pile. I tie the bag and hold it away from me.

I lean in the car. "What do I do with it?"

Nana's face wrinkles with disgust, but she also looks ready to laugh. "Throw it in the trunk for now. But we'd better not forget about it, or we'll be sorry next time we load up the groceries."

"Trust me. I'm never going to forget this." The trunk pops open, and I drop the bomb inside. When I get in the car, I use globs of hand sanitizer.

Nana is laughing now. "I can't believe what I just witnessed. Never in a million years."

"Must be a sign," I say, meeting her eyes in the rearview mirror. "A sign we should keep him."

She's not laughing anymore. "I'm sorry. We can't."

Pi lies down on the seat next to me and puts his head on my leg. There's no other dog I would do this for. He seems to know what I'm thinking. Without permission, my eyes fill with tears. And I have nothing sanitary to wipe them with.

I wish for a major traffic jam to stop our trip. We're not that lucky.

The animal control building comes into view on the right. I look down like I can prevent this from happening if I keep it out of sight. The car turns 2 times and then stops. Nana cuts the engine.

Pi squirms into my lap. He's shaking, and not in a tail-wagging happy way.

"I'm not ready. They're not open. Can we wait a few minutes?" My mouth shouts every thought that's flooding my brain. "I can't do this. Please. Maybe there's somewhere else. Please, don't. They're going to kill him."

"Lucy, honey, there's nothing we can do," Nana whispers. "I'm sorry."

My head is buried in Pi's fur. Nana lets me cry. I hear her get out of the car, and then I hear my door open. Her hand is on my shoulder. I wish for the digits of pi to sweep in, but all I feel is a trembling dog who will soon be gone.

"Lucy." The voice calling me is not Nana's. I look up at Windy. She's the 1 touching my shoulder. Her eyes are red and her cheeks spotty.

Levi stands behind her.

"What's going on?"

"We didn't think you should do this alone." Windy takes Pi from my lap.

"Thanks."

Levi pets Pi under his chin. Pi closes his eyes and stretches his neck. I know that he feels safe with us, and we are about to betray him.

"Take 5 minutes to say good-bye," Ms. Sitton says. "We need to get you to school."

"Okay," Windy says without argument.

There's a peeling bench in front of the building. Feeling weak, I take a seat doing my usual routine. Pi squirms free from Windy. He runs and dives into my lap.

All the air rushes from my lungs. "Whoa."

"Normally, I'd be jealous that he likes you more than me," Windy says. "But it's kind of a compliment because I picked you as a best friend, and Pi picked you as a best friend. He has good taste."

Levi groans and focuses his camera on Pi and me. But I won't need pictures to remember Pi.

Windy steps closer. Her voice is soft. "I'm going to miss you, Cutie Pi." She blows him a kiss.

Levi scratches Pi's chin 1 more time. "Bye, bud. You don't deserve ..." His voice quits on him.

Pi's tail beats against my leg. 1-2, 3-4, 5-6. His big, stupid eyes watch me. I look away to Levi and then to Windy.

"I don't know how to say good-bye." My throat has never been so dry and tight.

Pi whines softly as I cry.

Another car pulls into the lot. The tires crunch the gravel. Every second seems to be shooting by at top speed. Time won't stop. It's only getting faster.

"Is that Mr. Stoker?" Levi asks.

I look up and see our math teacher getting out of an SUV.

"Mr. Stoker? What are you doing here?" Windy asks. "Shouldn't you be in school?"

"I came to see about a dog."

A second ago, my chest hurt like I was being crushed by a boulder. Now it's flooding with hope, but I'm not ready to believe it.

"What are you talking about?" I ask.

He smiles and puts his hands in his pockets. He rocks back and forth. "Last night, I read on 1 of my favorite websites a moving post about a dog that needs a home."

"Pi's post has been up for 13 days," I remind him.

"Yeah, the pictures have been up forever," Levi adds.

"It wasn't on the Pet Hut page." Mr. Stoker looks at me.

"MathWhiz?" I ask.

"Yes," Mr. Stoker says. "My user name is—"

"SquareHead314?" Could I have been friends with a teacher?

"No. Don't laugh. It's MathMaster. I'm not really on that much."

I recognize the name. I always thought I deserved it. I even considered asking him/her to give it up. I was willing to math-duel for it.

"What's going on?" Windy's head turns from me to our teacher to me again.

I ignore her question. It can wait. Mine can't. "Are you really going to adopt Pi?"

"I'd like to. Is that okay?"

"Yes!" I yell, and Pi flinches. "Sorry." I give him a squeeze.

My head feels lighter, and I look up to the brilliant blue sky (the color of the number 4). I've never been so happy to solve a problem.

40

I'm sitting on the low brick wall outside East Hamlin Middle School, waiting for Nana. It's the last day of school before winter break, and we're heading to the airport to pick up Uncle Paul. Nana's thrilled. She was worried that he'd have to work over Christmas—or worse, that he'd be spending it with his girlfriend instead of with us.

"Guys, you don't have to wait with me," I say to Windy and Levi.

"We want to," Windy says. She *really* wants to share my bag of gumdrops.

"Whatever." Levi, who's shivering in his hooded sweatshirt, takes pictures of the bare tree branches. He's adding more nature shots to his photo collection on Art-Boom. But he prefers to focus on hidden beauty, like rotting pumpkins and stormy skies.

"Are you sure you can't go tonight?" Windy asks. She wants to go to the Pet Hut after school. Again. We've been there every day this week. The holidays are a busy time for pet adoption. I've plugged this new data into my formula. Dogs are being adopted 11 percent faster in December than in any other month.

"Not tonight. I haven't seen my uncle since October."

"Leave her alone," Levi says. "We'll all be there tomorrow."

My butt is numb from sitting on the freezing bricks. But the air gets even colder when Maddie walks by with her mom. I guess everyone is leaving early before the break.

"Hey," Windy says. But Maddie doesn't hear—or pretends not to hear.

Weeks ago, I'd apologized to Maddie for blowing up at her in math class. Judging by her silent response—and the fact that she got herself transferred to another math class—I think my apology was unaccepted. We're still together for 5 other classes, but we manage to never speak. Ever.

When her Cougars Care Project was featured on the local news 2 weeks ago, I almost told her congratulations. But I chickened out. Maddie, Jasmine, and Daniela deserved the spotlight. Their backpacks-for-refugees project was a huge success. (The reporter said they collected over 100 bags. I wish they knew the exact number.)

Telling Maddie that she means nothing to me, that she's a 0, was a crappy thing to do. I like to think that she forgot about it or doesn't care. But anytime I see her with glassy eyes, I wonder whether I had something to do with it. She has enough pressure without thinking about me and my stupid comments. We all have our problems.

At least Maddie's friends aren't so awful anymore. Jennifer and I were paired up in Spanish class for a project on a Latin American city. We had fun learning about Quito.

And even though I'm still in 7th-grade math and everyone—from the principal to all my classmates—knows I'm a savant, it's more or less okay. Mr. Stoker gives me extra work and projects. Math is still my favorite class, and language arts is still my least favorite. But I did like the unit on poetry. We had to count syllables! I volunteered to read a poem in front of the class. Ms. Fleming was very impressed.

Nana pulls up and waves. I give Windy a hug goodbye, along with the rest of the gumdrops.

"See ya tomorrow," I say to Levi.

"Yep."

As soon as I open the car door, I see the letter on the front seat. It's from NCASME. I grab it and then sit, stand, sit, stand, sit. I haven't even thought about my application for weeks. Just going back to school after my math-class incident was more than enough to worry about. For what seemed like forever, every murmur in class and in the hallways was about me. I wanted to leave. Finally, after Thanksgiving, the talk slowed and then stopped. It helped that some students hacked into the school's computer system. They weren't trying to change grades or cheat. They sent prank emails from Dr. Cobb that said things like East Hamlin was closed due to a smallpox outbreak. It was a big whodunit mystery for a whole week. An acquired savant can't compete with hackers.

Now, though, I have the letter in my hand, and I don't even know what I want it to say!

Nana smiles like she knows something, but the envelope is still sealed. I turn it over and over in my fingers.

"Aren't you going to open it?" she asks.

"Yeah."

She stares at me, and I keep fiddling. When a car honks behind us, she finally starts to drive away.

"Lucy, what are you waiting for?"

"I don't know."

"Even if you're accepted, you don't have to go. You can stay at your middle school." She pats my knee. "You know that."

"Don't you want me to go?" I ask.

"When the time is right."

I slide a finger under the flap of the envelope but stop. "How do you know when the time is right?"

"I don't." She laughs. "Not so easy to calculate. What I do know is, whenever you leave home—whether it's for the academy or Stanford—you'll leave a Lucy-sized hole in my heart. We won't be able to avoid that."

I stare out the window. Nana turns on the radio, and Christmas music fills the car. She's right: some things aren't easy to calculate. I put the letter in my backpack.

"Now what are you thinking about?" she asks. "You've got a goofy look on your face."

"Just adding some stuff in my head."

"You always are," she says with a little laugh.

But this time the math is different.

Since starting at East Hamlin, I've climbed the 55 steps in the school 232 times and counted all 950 lockers. I've grown ¾ of an inch and gained 6 pounds. I've had 77 math classes with 1 amazing teacher. I've read 2 books in language arts class (or 91,255 words). I've helped save 23 dogs so far and fallen in love with 1. I've even made 2 friends. I can add it all up, but the total doesn't begin to tell the story. As it turns out, I'm more than just numbers.

For the Love of Pi

- Pi is a mathematical constant. That means it's fixed. It won't change. We're stuck with it.
- Pi is represented by the Greek letter π, pronounced "pie."
- Pi is the relationship between a circle's circumference and its diameter.
- Circumference is the distance around the outside of a circle.
- Diameter is the distance across the circle, passing through the center.
- Pi is the circumference divided by the diameter.
- π = circumference ÷ diameter
- Or pi can be expressed like this:

$$\pi = \frac{circumference}{diameter} = 3.14159...$$

- Pi is the same for all circles, whether microscopic or gigantic.

- The digits in pi go on for infinity. There is no end or repeating pattern, so pi is called irrational.
- This is pi to the 500th decimal place:
3.14159265358979323846264338327950288419716939
93751058209749445923078164062862089986280348
25342117067982148086513282306647093844609550
58223172535940812848111745028410270193852110
55596446229489549303819644288109756659334461
28475648233786783165271201909145648566923460
34861045432664821339360726024914127372458700
66063155881748815209209628292540917153643678
92590360011330530548820466521384146951941511
60943305727036575959195309218611738193261179
31051185480744623799627495673518857527248912
2793818301194912
- But it is common to round pi to as little as 3.14.
- A circle with a diameter of 1 has a circumference of 1π.
- A circle with a diameter of 2 has a circumference of 2π.
- A circle with a diameter of 88 has a circumference of 88π.
- A circle with a diameter of 9,727,360 has a circumference of 9,727,360π.
- The day to celebrate pi, perhaps with a slice of pie, is March 14. Get it? 3/14.
- Pi is a great name for a dog.

All About Fibonacci

Lucy sees math all around her—and not just digits, though she loves those, too. The shapes that make our world can often be calculated. Lucy's favorite example of this is the Fibonacci sequence, which can be graphed as an approximate spiral and found in nautilus seashells, seed patterns in a sunflower, the arrangement of petals in a rose, hurricanes, the bracts of a pinecone, and spiral galaxies. These are nature's masterpieces, and Lucy hangs this art in her bedroom.

The Fibonacci sequence is a series of numbers that begins with 0 and 1 and where every number that follows is the sum of the 2 numbers before it.

0, 1

So the next number would be 0 + 1.

0, 1, 1

The next would be 1 + 1.

0, 1, 1, 2

Then 1 + 2. And it can go infinitely.

0, 1, 1, 2, 3, 5, 8, 13, 21, 34, 55, 89, 144, 233, 377, 610, 987, 1597, 2584, 4181, 6765, 10946, 17711, 28657, 46368, 75025, 121393, 196418, 317811, 514229, 832040, 1346269 . . .

When the Fibonacci sequence is drawn as a set of blocks, these squares can be used to create an approximate spiral.

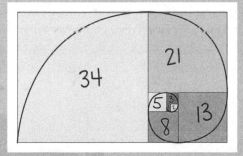

- The day to celebrate Fibonacci is November 23. Get it? 11/23.
- While Pi is a great name for a dog, Fibonacci might be a good name for a cat.

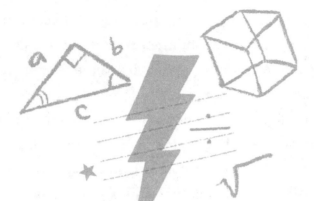

The Thank-You Section

As I sit down to write this, I'm going to estimate that there are at least 50 people I need to thank for making this book (and my dreams!) a reality. Let's see if I calculated correctly.

1 & 2: Lori Kilkelly (world's best agent) and Paul Rodeen of Rodeen Literary Management. Lori, thanks for plucking me from the slush pile in 2013 and being my champion and friend ever since. Your patience and care for this book elevated the story. Here's to long hours,

hard work, gluten-free options, celebrations, and the Green Bay Packers.

3: My editor at Random House Books for Young Readers, Caroline Abbey, whose passion for *MLG* was evident from the beginning. Luckily, the hearts in the manuscript margins continued draft after draft. Caroline, thank you for caring deeply about these characters and pushing for the best book.

4–10: The Random House team behind the book, including Michelle Nagler, Maria Middleton, Kathy Dunn, Jenna Lisanti, Julie Conlon, Kristin Schulz, and Barbara Bakowski (sorry for all. the. math.). The enthusiasm for *MLG* could not be topped. Thank you for believing in this book, making it the best it could be, and launching it into the world.

11 & 12: Carolyn Coman and Stephen Roxburgh, the best writing teachers and indie editors in the world. *Can you believe this is actually happening?* This book would not be possible without you.

13–20: My writing buddies Laura Gehl, Peter McCleery, Camille Andros, Lori Richmond, Megan Bryant, Tara Luebbe, Jason Gallaher, and Anthony Piraino. You are my coworkers. I love this job, but having you with me (mostly virtually, but sometimes in real life) makes it merrier.

21–23: Sharon Kolling-Perin, Caleb Kolling-Perin,

and Dr. Jennifer Gagné. Thank you for offering your insights into OCD. You made this book better and more authentic. Any mistakes or inconsistencies are my fault alone.

24–27: Daniel Tammet, Darold A. Treffert, and Jason Padgett and Maureen Seaberg, all of whom wrote fascinating books about savant syndrome.

28 & 29: Dr. Nancy Wrinkle Molden and Natalie Strange, for expanding my math world.

30: Rebecca Vanarsdall at the Mathematical Association of America (MAA.org). Check out its site for all things math.

31–34: My moral support team of Jen Black, Julie Hamilton, Mabel Cameron, and Penny Nichols. You are who I turn to when I need anything, especially a laugh.

35 & 36: Delaney Black and Laura Gruszka, for reading early drafts.

37: Kate Beasley, for the first blurb and the sweetest, most supportive email I've ever received.

38–43: Lin-Manuel Miranda, Tina Fey, Amy Poehler, Mayim Bialik, Oprah, and John Oliver. When I'm taking a break from writing, these are the creative minds that entertain me. (And if I'm being honest, maybe by mentioning them, I'll get to meet these brilliant folks someday.)

44: My dad, who loves all books, says nice things about me behind my back, and encouraged me to be an engineer. (He also thought I should consider acting, though, because he doesn't believe in limiting oneself.)

45: My mom! Supportive from day 1—meaning, since the day I was born.

46–56: And more family—Suzanne, Glen, Bob and Fran, Kristen (idea-generating genius!) and Andy, Frank and Stacey, Brian and Jess, and Gram.

57–59: In memory of Pepper—for nearly nine years she was my office mate and furry baby. And Jack and Munchkin, who keep me company while I write, often under my desk, on my feet (just like Pi). I'd be lost without my K9 support team.

60: Henry, my funny boy who has promised to be a neuroscientist when he grows up, because I'm obsessed with the human brain. (Though at this point he'd prefer to be a YouTube star.)

61: Lily, who after reading an early draft cried for Lucy and then gave me the silent treatment for being mean to my character. That was incredibly encouraging.

62: Cora, for reading this book more times than anyone else, and creating fan art, and *shipping* Levi and Lucy from the 1st draft. And for helping me solve the Putnam problem. It only took us a few hours, working together, to do what Lucy did in 15 minutes.

63: Brett. For everything! I love you.

Well, it was 63. Looks like I was off by 26 percent.

A few final, immeasurable thanks:

∞ To teachers, librarians, booksellers, parents, and anyone who puts books into the hands of young readers. Thank you! And a special shout-out to these booksellers for the early love: Abby Rauscher, Janelle Smith, Joanna Albrecht, Colleen Regan, Margaret Brennan Neville, Dea Lavoie, Carol Moyer, Kira Wizner, and Leslie Hawkins.

∞ And thank YOU, Reader (with a capital R). This book is for you.

About the Author

Stacy McAnulty is an award-winning author of 8 picture books and 8 chapter books. She worked as a mechanical engineer for 8 years before becoming a writer. Originally from 12054 (NY), Stacy now lives in 27284 (NC) with her 3 kids, 3 dogs, 1 husband, and 1 goldfish (for a total of 8 roommates). *The Miscalculations of Lightning Girl* is her 1st novel. To learn more, visit stacymcanulty.com or find her on social media:

Twitter: @stacymcanulty
Instagram: StacyMcAnulty
Facebook: StacyMcAnultyAuthor